2884—
Ixodia Escape

by
T.A. Sankar

PublishA
Balti

PublishAmerica has allowed this work to remain exactly as the author intended, verbatim, without editorial input.

Softcover: 978-1-60749-411-9
PUBLISHED BY PUBLISHAMERICA, LLLP
www.publishamerica.com
Baltimore

Printed in the United States of America

*To my wife Tara and children
Tarika, Aleksander and Arianna,
who have enriched my life in indescribable ways.*

2884—
Ixodia Escape

PROLOGUE

The year was 435.027 and in three days time, schools all over the populated System would be on break for the next month.

Actually by the calendar of the Originals—it was January 27th, 2884 as they preferred to count time in the Old Earth's calendar. Both the Lunites, people native to the moon, and the Voyagers, those who lived in Space Stations prefer to use the New Calendar. They used the last day on Earth—December 31st 2448 as the end of the Weapons Age and January 1st, 2449 as Day One of the new time period. It was that day, that mass exodus from Earth took place. It was that day that the population of Space Stations and the moon grew *one hundred fold*. And it was the previous day that more than ninety percent of the Earth's population perished.

The new time period had ushered in changes that were unthinkable in the 25th century. They were well into the fifth century now. Mars was populated by both Lunites and Voyagers. They lived relatively peacefully as they shared resources based on numerous treaties that rarely needed enforcement in recent times. Over the last 100 years, almost all children from the System beyond the age of eight went to school on Earth as it had the benefit of resources that neither the Lunites nor Voyagers possessed.

In the last 50 years or so, it was strongly encouraged, though not mandatory, that all classes had a mixture of Lunites, Voyagers and Originals.

It was about one and one half years ago, seemingly like an eternity, since Xander, Jelina, Arielle and Mondeus met on their first day of school in that ever expanding beautiful Caribbean Island that hosted the Plato system of schools. It seemed as if it were a random event, as classes were in groups of eight, usually four Originals and any combination of Lunites and Voyagers. The well supervised system of assignment by a central computer was pretty much final with parameters of eight students per class every two years, at least four Originals and equal amount of boys and girls. Xander and Jelina were siblings and hence the formula was slightly altered—not an unusual request from Lunites or Voyagers at the time who wanted to keep families together as far as possible. After their first few months of school they always went on vacation together. The anticipation of their third long break coming up soon made it very difficult to concentrate on the final days of testing. School year 15A was coming to a close for them, 16A for Xander.

The reason for their unusual excitement was very simple. For the first time they would be able to *leave* the system without an accompanying adult. They were going to the Ixodia system for vacation. Xander, who was now 16, had just obtained his spaceship license. He could be accompanied by up to five people over the age of 14 in a craft providing that he reported to Central Station every forty eight hours during travel. Jelina and Arielle were both 15. Mondeus, a genius of sorts, was almost 15 but not quite. Still he was well beyond 14 and as such they could all go away for an *entire* three weeks together before going home for another week. Then it would be back to school, for year 15B.

PART I
The System

I.

"Xander, please make sure you tuck him in bed," teased Arielle.

"I will but I am not reading him any bedtime Alien stories," replied Xander coyly.

"I am sure a few fairy tales would do," Arielle added playfully.

"I'll think of something," said Xander trying to keep the peace before bedtime.

"It will soon be midnight, Cinderella," retorted Mondeus from his quarters. "Let's see how you'll look in the morning."

Mondeus had already turned in and was sleepy at 21.00 hours. Despite not having a travel day, the four friends were just approaching the Rings of Saturn and were still well within the System and its numerous outposts. They were planning to get to the main Launch station orbiting Neptune on Day 1 of vacation time. They had used their travel day, which is the extra day of odd months of the year, to get an early start to their vacation. This was January 31st, 2884 by the

Originals calendar. It was 435.031 by that of the Lunites and Voyagers.

"Jelina, could you switch to maintenance power before you go to sleep? Decrease gravity by fifty percent and dim lights if you turn in before 22.00, as the automatic settings will kick in at that time," Xander said. "I want to get some rest before our launch tomorrow."

"I know, I know," said Jelina. She was a bit nervous as this would be Xander's first trip as lead pilot outside the system. Xander did not seem to be the least bit perturbed and seemed quite relaxed and calm as if he had done this many times before. Actually Xander got an almost perfect score getting a total of 49.8 in 50 simulations. He was also assistant pilot on a short trip out of the System in the last six months.

He could hear Arielle giggling from the room across the hallway that she shared with his sister Jelina. He also knew that they were not going to get to sleep before 22.00 and his caution to change to power efficient settings were just words. It seemed as if young teenagers always had too much to talk about. He liked to hear her giggle but for now he knew he needed to get some rest. He tapped the control panel at the head of his bed and the door closed soundlessly. Mondeus was already fast asleep. The low drone of the engine of the Pelican 25 was the last thing he heard before slipping into a deep sleep.

II.

Startled, Xander jumped up in bed suddenly. For a split second he did not know where he was. The staccato movement of the spacecraft was completely unexpected. The Level One emergency lights came on but no alarm sounded.

"What's happening?" Jelina asked tersely, her voice coming over the intercom with concern that was thinly veiled.

Almost at the same time Mondeus, still half sleeping worriedly inquired "This couldn't be a wormhole already, could it?"

"Not this soon," Xander said flatly as his brain engaged. "We are still in the System. There are no wormholes in the System."

The movements of the spacecraft felt as if one were fully awake going through a wormhole in normal environmental settings. The Originals likened it to early 20th century air travel with severe turbulence. Such movements were usually caused by large pressure variations in the path of rapid travel.

A full five seconds had passed and Xander had not come up with a reason for this unexpected severe turbulence that actually seemed to be getting worse by the deci-second. Still, to their surprise, no alarm sounded from the Pelican 25.

The Pelican series of spacecrafts were the safest and most stable in the history of space travel. They were almost fully automated and were highly recommended for junior pilots. One could plot a course at base, have it approved and engraved at Central station, and virtually spend only about ten minutes per day at the controls, for a trip of a month's duration.

The girls were in Xander and Mondeus's room now. They had rushed over during the commotion. The secondary controls were located on this level of the ship. The main controls were, of course, at the central deck of the ship with an extension into the apex of the ship that made it easier for it to be reached remotely.

Arielle tried to hide her concern but her voice betrayed it. "Xander, we couldn't be out of the system yet, could we?"

"No, our largest closest body is still Saturn as you can see via the main video panel," Xander calmly stated. The staccato movement had gotten worse and even though Xander was calm his speech was slightly hurried. Arielle knew that he spoke more words per second when he was anxious, a fact that did nothing to relieve her concern.

"I got it," Mondeus stated emphatically. He was now fully awake, his voice coming from the corner of the room. Just as he said this, the turbulence all but ceased.

"What is it?" Xander asked.

Mondeus who rarely showed much emotion when sitting in front of a computer screen, was sitting poker faced at the terminals on his side of the room. Even though he was nearly two years younger than Xander and officially third in command of this spacecraft, Xander had learnt to respect his opinion over time. He was poring over their original travel plans and had zoned into the micro environment of their present location.

"Illuminate the exterior and set the windows to Telescope settings 10. Anywhere from 10 to 15 will do," Mondeus instructed.

Xander tapped the buttons for the lights to decrease in the interior of the ship. This would enable them to see outside. It was just about 2.00 hours and it was quite bright, relatively speaking. As he adjusted the windows to telescopic settings, he said, "Eureka."

The girls looked at him relieved and Mondeus nodded in agreement. They had the most incredible view of almost all the rings of Saturn. From the inside of the rings! When Xander's father had plotted this course, he had recommended a brief sightseeing stop from the innermost rings of Saturn. And he had discussed this with Xander. So focused was Xander on his first trip as lead pilot out of the System that it had slipped him momentarily. The innermost rings of Saturn had a huge magnetic field that often caused turbulence to passing crafts. It was expected and that was the reason no alarm went off in the Pelican 25.

For a moment Xander grinned sheepishly. However, he quickly regained his authoritative voice and said, "Because we made such good time, we caught the field in our sleep cycle. We were expected to be at this point just at the beginning of our wake cycle but we made use of the drag of Jupiter and were ahead of our expected arrival time. We can afford an extra 30 minutes to enjoy the view."

He tapped on another button and decreased their gravity to 30 per cent of normal. It gave them that nice billowing, floating on clouds feeling. He knew that Arielle loved these settings because the Lunites tended to prefer less gravity. It seemed to be hardwired into them. Voyagers on the other hand adjusted their settings as frequently as they adjusted their temperatures. Mondeus tried as often as possible to keep his feet firmly on the ground. Literally and figuratively.

The view outside was stunningly beautiful. Thousands upon thousands of concentric rings around them. In what seemed like millions of shades of colors. Initially there was a breathtaking awe and wonderment. As their breathing returned to normal, there came a more inexpressible calming feeling of reverence. It was like staring at millions of distant stars on a dark night only one thousand times more intense. As they kept looking at this awe inspiring spectacle, they became enveloped and absorbed into it. Bodily desires of hunger and thirst quickly diminished and seem to fade into insignificance. The sheer magnitude of this spectacle humbled them, rendered them almost irrelevant. Into tiny, miniscule beings. Like afterthoughts of an artist brush, adding specks of paints on a giant sized painting. Not sure whether they enhanced or intruded. Feeling like the size of a dust particle in a sandstorm. *Which in reality is much larger than what we are, in this vast Universe,* Xander reflected.

Xander's father knew that this needed to be experienced to be understood. His description of it to his children would be woefully inadequate. In fact, many of life's most pleasurable feelings needed to be experienced to be understood as words do them no justice. How does one describe the feeling of a bathing under a waterfall on a rocky ledge in a rainforest? How does one describe the calm, multi-colored methane seas in the outer bodies of the System or tranquil, aquamarine waters of the Southern Caribbean Sea? Words cannot suffice. Such was the spectacle from the inner rings of Saturn. Indescribably beautiful and magnificent. Humbling indeed.

III.

"We will be picked up in a few minutes," Mondeus said matter-of-factly.

"OK, I will take over for now," stated Xander.

"I can do it."

"It is better if I do. We cannot take the risk of having negative log points. It can affect our future travel plans."

"OK, I will observe keenly," Mondeus conceded, choosing his words carefully.

"Five minutes and twenty seconds for contact with Central Station," Xander said using his clinical voice and informing Jelina and Arielle at the same time.

They were still several hundred thousand miles from the massive Central station that orbited Neptune. Ships were detected this far out and channeled to the respective ports. As soon as Central Station detected a ship its computers latch on to that of the ship's computers after matching the previously filed and approved flight plans. It then creates a magnetic channel into which the ship is guided and other ships cannot enter. It can, of course, be manually overridden but the need to do this arises in less than one in a million flights. As the ship gets closer to the Stations and the traffic is more intense, the magnetic field is stronger and it is more difficult to get out of the channels. Almost all ships these days have induced repulsive magnetic properties that are inversely proportional to the distance from another ship, making collision almost impossible. With the vastly increased traffic in the System in recent decades these measures were necessary to prevent chaos and accidents.

"We're fully locked in now," said Xander. He had not touched a button nor issued a command to the controls but the screen displayed that their small homely craft was being channeled and everything was going as expected.

"Easy as ABC," murmured a voice from behind him. Jelina and Arielle had come over to his control station as they were approaching Central Station. "It's not everyday that one gets to dock at Central station." On their screen they could see massive spacecrafts of numerous designs that were being channeled as well.

"How long is our stopover time?" asked Arielle.

"Two hours max," simultaneously articulated Xander and Mondeus.

"Enough to go sightseeing and quick shopping?" inquired Arielle.

"Depends on how quickly we are processed," Xander replied.

"Oh, I was hoping that I could get a few gifts from the shops here for my friends." Arielle had a hint of disappointment in the tone of her voice.

"Don't worry, you will have tons of opportunities to buy all you want in the Ixodia system," ventured Jelina. "In fact, I am pretty sure you would have used up all your credits and will be trying to borrow some of mine before we are midway through our vacation," she added.

"Not this time."

"You always do."

They were getting very close to the Central station now and it was visible on the video screen with hardly any telescopic power. What a grinning monstrosity! It was a massive structure with countless arms protruding into all directions and then shorter arms attached to those arms as they faded into the distance. It was a maze and a marvel at the same time. An enormous intricate structure that was engineered with functionality as its prime objective but definitely not an eyesore. Maybe the utter magnitude of it prevented one from thinking that it could actually be ugly. In fact, it could be described as gargantuan which seemed to be lower on the glamour scale than colossal. Regardless, there was no comparable structure in the entire System.

The VIPs always got preference for the innermost ports. The Pelican had gotten a spot in the innermost 20% of one of the central arms. Not bad for a small craft. Most likely due to the fact that flight plans were filed very early—courtesy of Xander's father. Being a distant galaxy astronomer may also have its benefits as Xander's and Jelina's father frequently passed though here.

The biggest advantage of having an inner port is the fact that they were usually manned. Sure robots performed most of the duties but it was nice to have that personal touch of humans. The vast majority of people who worked here were Voyagers. They seem to be least bothered by lesser gravity and pretty much continuous artificial lighting. Centuries of adaptation, perhaps.

"Wow," Arielle exclaimed. "Did you see that huge ship?"

"Yeah. Our ship could fit into one of their closets," Mondeus replied.

"I once saw a ship larger than that one but I've never seen so many large ships in one place," Xander added.

They could now see hundreds of crafts all around them with the naked eye. The majority were larger than theirs. Some were humongous. Likely due to the fact that they were now in the inner arms of Central station. They were pretty much locked into this channel as more elaborate ships glided by. The lighting improved around them—artificial, of course. The Pelican 25 came to a standstill. Almost. Then a slight movement at 90 degrees to their original path. A few sounds and they were locked in. The instruments showed that they were properly docked. Quickly and efficiently.

"We are here!" Xander announced, stating the obvious.

"We can all see that Commander," teased Arielle.

"That's it?" a half question, half statement from Mondeus. He was a tad disappointed. He thought that their docking would be a bit more exciting. In his logical mind, he knew the process was fully automated and all they were required to do was to monitor the controls. In the event of something not going according to plan—it would be picked up quickly.

"I could have been sleeping," Mondeus said.

They all knew that Mondeus was not going to miss docking at Central station for anything. Yet he was an unusual contradiction. Externally he was not very emotive and expressive. Internally he loved excitement, yet he never showed much of it.

"Doors will be open in three minutes," Xander instructed.

As if one cue the girls rushed over to their quarters for two minutes of grooming and another to pick up their travel bag.

"Can't wait for us to get into the worm holes," muttered Mondeus.

"You'll be at Level 2 conscious level and won't know a thing," said Xander pointing out the obvious. Mondeus knew this but still had a bit of a scowl on his face, residual from a most mundane docking. Xander could not help but grin. He would be the only one at Level 4 conscious level until they got past the Oort Cloud. Then he would join them at Level 2 for the rest of the trip through the pathways to Ixodia. For reasons unclear, these Pathways in space were still referred to as wormholes by almost all except astronomers. Even though they did not remotely resemble a wormhole. Remnants of old English, he supposed.

With barely a sound the two adjacent doors of the Pelican 25 opened simultaneously with that of their docking gallery. They were now staring directly at one of the numerous processing rooms of the massive station. The equipment looking back at them was not all that familiar and seemed oddly out of place.

"Welcome." A non-automated human voice with no source immediately identifiable floated in to greet them.

IV.

"Captain Xander Rael Villanova," the unidentified voice continued "you and your crew may disembark."

It was the first time he had really heard someone refer to him as captain since the day he obtained his spacecraft license. It sounded distinctly unfamiliar. And for his full name to be called out—that often caused a bit of subconscious apprehension as his father usually did this when he was much younger and in trouble.

"Yes madam," Xander said finding his voice after a brief moment.

"Thank you," he continued.

Xander, followed by Jelina, Mondeus and Arielle entered the docking gallery. The room was large but appeared larger than it really was because of a complex system of mirrors. It was octagonal in shape and had two smaller enclosures that blended into the overall shape. The lighting seemed to reflect on the walls at unusual angles. They knew that these rooms could be quickly opened into larger areas depending on the amount of passengers needing to be processed. It goes without saying that they could be observed through the walls because the system of lighting could allow the mirrors to be one way i.e. a mirror when they were looking into it but a transparent window from the other side. However, this technique was rarely employed unless one had a previous record of not abiding with the laws in the System.

Standing there to greet them was a very tall beautiful young woman. She was dressed in a single piece uniform with a badge indicating that she worked for Outer System Security. Because of her height, they guessed she was Lunite. She seemed almost too young to be serving in this position. Mondeus stared and Xander wanted to but thought it would not be polite. Not to mention that Arielle always observed him closely under these situations. Her assured mannerism quickly dispelled any thoughts about her experience. Her voice was welcoming yet professional in manner.

"I trust that you have had a good and uneventful flight so far."

"We did," they all said almost simultaneously.

Arielle wanted to add that they had a minor scare through the rings of Saturn but quickly decided against it as no one else spoke up. Flights within the System were relatively low speed affairs and usually uneventful. Common courtesies still dictated that one inquired, regardless.

"We should be able to get you out of here in half of an hour if there are no issues with your clearance," she continued. Again the voice was so smooth that it sounded as it were a professional recording on a voice machine.

"We have been trying to improve on our turnaround time to accommodate the extra traffic during the school break," she explained.

The girls exchanged looks. Without uttering a word, they both realized that shopping at Central Station was entirely out of the question. Oh well, perhaps they could on their trip back into the System. One minor hurdle though, they would most likely used up all their credits on vacation and not able to buy anything! Then they would have to settle for window shopping.

"That would be great. We can then have an extra hour in Ixodia," Xander agreed politely.

The girls scowled at him. Mondeus appeared indifferent as usual.

"OK, let's get started then," she said.

Xander wondered what her name was as he did not recall her saying anything. She did not have to, of course. As if reading his mind and on cue, she said "I am Gianette. You may call me Gian."

"Xander will need a Level 8 clearance. For the rest a Level 7 is adequate. If Jelina wants to be listed as the sole co-captain she would also need a Level 8."

Jelina quickly spoke up, "Level 7 is fine, as Mondeus is occasionally co captain."

The level headed Jelina was also considerate. She knew that even though she had more experience than Mondeus he was very flattered to be joint co-captain and took his role very seriously. He looked up to Xander and considered himself on par with the girls. Reminding him of his younger status was a sensitive subject to him though truth be told, he was just as capable as they were in most matters.

"You will all be together for the first part of the clearance. The higher level for Xander just requires one additional step," she informed them.

"Follow me please," she instructed as she walked briskly to one of the enclosures that housed two large headed robots. The large heads were, of course, intricate computers. Those models were a bit older now as the recent models had much smaller but no less intricate computers.

As they crossed over the threshold into the enclosure, the robots quickly started to issue instructions.

"Stand here," one robot directed.

"Place your hands over here," another instructed.

"Open your eyes fully for three seconds," the instructions continued.

"Place your chin here on this platform and stay still for five seconds."

"Thank you."

"Next, please."

The robots went over the exact routine again.

Small red lights blinked as it entered data. It hissed softly as data was being processed and continued with it programmed monotonous routine.

"Thank you."

The voices were clearly robotic but you if were not fully alert it could be mistaken for a human voice, so good had these machines become. The arms of the robots moved up and down quickly making soft mechanical sounds. The sequence was uninterrupted and the entire process lasted just a few minutes for all four of them.

The clearance was fairly simple. First a hand scan was done that was inclusive of all ten finger patterns. This was followed by a retinal scan.

And lastly a radiographic pattern of the bony structures of the face was taken. These were all matched to the stored identification data for each person. Unless, there was a mismatch, the routine was then complete.

"Xander, you may come over here," Gian instructed. Xander needed to get an additional step in the clearance process. This was a DNA analysis that was required for Level 8 clearance. The other robot in the far corner of the room issued instructions for this step. This time the process was closely observed by Gian.

In short, it consisted of pressing a sterile microscopic slide on the moistened lips of the subject. Enough cells were present in the small amount of saliva on the slide. The robot then performed a DNA identification analysis and matched it to its database. After almost a minute, it said "positive identification made."

Gian nodded. She had programmed their information in prior to their arrival and with the scans and DNA analysis done—they all had the green light to go as the robots had efficiently done their jobs as always. The matches in the computers also served as a log that the four passengers were at this station at the stated time. The accuracy was believed to be 100%.

"You may reboard and start your sequence for hyperspace travel as soon as you desire," Gian stated pretty much indicating that clearance had been given and this docking was over.

"Thank you," they all said again.

And with a knowing smile Gian added, "And best wishes for your vacation."

Young teenagers these days, she thought to herself. They all wanted to go out of the system for their time off from school. They almost made it seem like a requirement. The young never seem to do what one expects of them. Always trying to expand their horizons. Testing their boundaries. Even if it were not in their best interests. It seemed as if it were a basic need of humans. As basic as food and air.

V.

As the multi layered door of the Pelican 25 slid to a close, it suddenly dawned upon them that the real trip and vacation was about to begin. There was a sense of quiet excitement. It seemed as if, without planning to, no one had really let their guard down until now. The local part of their trip, the Intra System travel was now completed. The next step was preparation for, and travel through, hyperspace.

"We have about 30 minutes until we begin the sequence," Xander said.

"We will go a few thousand miles away from the station and float there before we drop conscious levels."

He confirmed the program with the ship computers as they glided quickly away from the heavy traffic, opting for a quiet spot to relax before going under. He knew central station would provide any medical help, if needed, as they prepared for the high speed travel in the pathways.

Even though they had all been outside the System before, this would be their first trip to Ixodia. Not to mention there was no adult supervising them going through the Pathways. This time Xander was in charge. It was very exciting but sort of scary at the same time. A bit of anxiety was definitely part of that feeling of exhilaration.

"Captain Xander, can we stay awake with you until the Oort Cloud?" Arielle joked, trying to make light conversation.

Arielle wasn't really looking for an answer since she knew that was not part of the normal flight plans. Mondeus answered anyway.

"Only one person is needed to monitor the controls until we lose all gravitational pull from the Sun. He also has to dodge the last of the comets. It is a safety recommendation."

"I know, I know dodo head," Arielle chided.

"Just in case you forgot, pretty face," Mondeus countered.

"OK boy genius."

"Thank you, thank you very much," Mondeus said in his best Elvis impression.

Xander was looking over the flight charts for the umpteenth time. Jelina was sitting on a chair with one elbow propping up her chin from the low table, feet resting on another chair. She noted their idle banter without really digesting it. This was common place between these two and was more often than not, amusing. She often wondered why Mondeus responded to the idle comments from Arielle when he would rarely respond to similar comments from the others. Or perhaps, Jelina did not make as many carefree comments as the rest of them. Even now, staring out of one of the many windows of the Pelican 25, she appeared oddly reflective and didn't seem to notice what she was looking at.

Jelina was the best friend anyone could have. She had developed a very close friendship with Arielle that began when they first met. Strange enough Arielle was the bubbly one who usually talked much more. Whilst by no means introverted, Jelina was often quiet until she got to know someone well. Maybe it was just her cautious nature. No doubt this had something to do with her growing up without her mother, whom she last saw when she was five years old.

Like Jelina's father, her mother was also a distant galaxy astronomer. She did a lot of work related travel but was home with the kids for long intervals in between travel. On one of these missions, she and her small crew were reported as missing. Just lost communication with all systems. Vanished. Literally into the thin air. It was a few days before this was communicated to them. Xander's father knew earlier but was still hopeful that they would be located. As time went on, hope gradually faded but they never completely gave up. To this day, they still held out a faint hope that she may be alive.

Under the circumstances, Jelina had to grow up a bit more quickly than she normally would have. Even though she last saw her mother nine years ago—she still remembered her vividly. She did not need video images and visigraphs as the memories of her mother were always crystal clear. It was a subject that she and Xander rarely discussed these days. It was too painful to revisit.

Xander's father was a rock to them. He tried very hard to make up for the loss of their mother—sometimes too hard. He was always there for them. He did as much as possible with them and they were very very close to him. Sometimes, they forgot that his loss was just as great as theirs. So far, he had not remarried.

Maybe it was something about boys. Outwardly Xander never showed any signs that his family and upbringing was anything but normal. The same could not be said about Jelina. It had molded her personality. She was more quiet and grounded. Only people very close to her saw her true colors. She confided in Arielle. One could never figure why as their personalities were quite contrasting. Maybe there are still undiscovered forces that dictate whom we learn to trust and get close to. Whatever the reasons, Arielle, a Lunite and Jelina, a Voyager, were extremely close. They could communicate at times without even saying a word. Just by being able to sense each other's moods.

Arielle sensed that Jelina wanted to be left alone as she was deep in her own thoughts. Perhaps it was preparing to travel through the pathways that set Jelina thinking again. Perhaps travel of this nature would always remind her of the loss of her mother. It was too early to tell. Such situations persisting into adulthood could affect her close relationships.

Travels through the pathways were commonplace now. The risks were very small but they still existed. Concerns were never proportional to the actual risks of travel but just the fact that there were risks, no matter how small, could cause trepidation. The concerns, of course, varied widely amongst individuals. The paranoid ones had them blown entirely out of proportion and the carefree ones never gave them a second thought. Naturally, none of these really changed the actual degree of risk.

Jelina, known to be intuitive, could not quite place what she was feeling. It was neither worry nor sadness. It was an unusual sense of apprehension. The type that cannot be explained with facts alone. She seemed to sense that something was not well but could not put her finger on it. She did not want to share this with the others because there was no evidence to support that anything at all was amiss. Not the least of which, she did not want to trouble Xander unnecessarily. This was a very big event for him.

His voice brought her back to reality.

"Five minutes to cooling time," he instructed.

"Already?" asked Mondeus.

"We can't wait, Captain Xander," said Arielle as she tried to make light matter of the subject.

"You'll need to be in the pressure stations in three minutes. Sedation begins one minute prior to cooling," Xander continued, not seeing much humor in the present situation.

"We are ready Xander," Jelina offered calmly, as usual.

VI.

Xander stared at the panels of instruments. They were traveling very quickly away from the system but not nearly as fast as they would soon be traveling when they entered the Pathways.

He then looked over to his side. His sister Jelina, Arielle and Mondeus appeared to be sleeping peacefully sitting in their chairs. The specially designed chairs were at a 25 degree incline and they were not really sleeping in the real sense of the word. They were in a transparent chamber that was connected to the compartment in which Xander was sitting and their level of consciousness was being decreased stepwise.

Firstly, there was mild sedation—anesthetic gases infused at the programmed time. The chamber was then cooled gradually. This was barely uncomfortable as their specially designed thermal suits gave them a sense of comfort whilst they were still fully conscious. As the gradual cooling was taking place, the pressure in the chamber was increased—all preprogrammed for hyperspace travel after the sequences were initiated.

Xander was undergoing the same process but with minimal sedation and much less pressure and cooling. This would be delayed until almost another hour when he would undergo the full process just prior to entering the Pathways. At this stage he could still override the automatic processes if needed. This need arose just about once in more than a thousand trips. Mainly to make slight adjustments if the ship sensors detected unexpected comets or floating debris in its flight path, in the Oort cloud.

Xander's compartment environment would be identical to that of his companions prior to Pathway travel. As well as his condition.

With everyone else asleep, Xander being only slightly sedated and the instruments showing nothing out of the ordinary, he was left with some time for thinking. He could easily communicate with Central Station but there was no need for that. In previous trips outside the system, he would have already been at Level 2 consciousnesses and hence did not know he had this much time to kill. He looked at the clock again. He had 42 minutes before entering the Pathways. That seemed to be a very long time now. He could initiate his sequence a bit earlier and hope that all went well with the ship guidance system but he was a responsible young man and usually played by the rules. Hence, he would keep vigil until it was absolutely necessary for him to go under.

OK, he thought, *if I start the sequence five minutes prior to the entry of the pathways, I would still have another 37 minutes of staring at the others and the instrument panel.* Xander finally felt a bit lonely. He tried to keep his mind occupied and to focus on the task at hand but his thoughts kept drifting off.

Maybe it was that touch of sedation. Maybe it was just the fact that his friends and sister were less that 10 feet away from him but he could not talk to them. Even if they were reversed it would take several minutes to bring them back up safely. So they were here but he was essentially alone. He did not imagine it this way. He had figured being awake for less than an hour whilst the others were under—would be a brief time. Especially with him having the responsibility of captaining the ship without any help. But the computers ran everything. There was not much to do.

Still 33 minutes minimum for him to go under. Xander was definitely restless now. The panels showed that they were accelerating faster than ever. They had not come within several hundred thousand miles of any icy rocks and were approaching the outer limits of pull from the system.

"I think he would make an excellent medical doctor," he had heard his mother saying.

"I wouldn't mind if he followed our footsteps," Dr Balkan Villanova had replied.

"He has a lot of time to decide what he wants to but I don't want him to feel obligated that he needs to be an astronomer like us, to live up to our expectations," she continued.

"The final choice will be ultimately up to him," Dr Villanova had assured her.

"I know, I know, my dear," murmured Xander and Jelina's mother.

"I am still not sure," Xander muttered out loud. One of the decisions that Xander would soon face would be whether to attend University on Earth or on one of the Space Stations, as his father did. Clearly his father's University was renown in the field of distant-galaxy astronomy and it would be a great choice for Xander if he did indeed chose this field of study. However, if he chose the medical field, he would likely stay on Earth.

He was surprised to hear his own voice in the stillness of the Pelican 25 control center. He did not think it was audible and he was responding to a scene that took place almost nine years ago when he had stumbled upon his parents discussing his possible future and career. They had quickly ended the conversation and at the time it seemed like a trifling thing. He was not aware that parents thought about their children's career and future so early in their life. Maybe some do. Maybe all do but many never really vocalized it. Maybe they would have done this on many more occasions in the future had his mother's fate permitted it. Regardless, he had come to reflect on that particular conversation many times over the years. And still he did not have a clear idea of what profession he wanted to choose for the rest of his life.

Dr Villanova was not a medical doctor. Because of the heights he had reached in his field he was conferred this honorary title. He had obtained this title at a relatively early age. Both of Xander and Jelina's parents were astute and well accomplished distant galaxy astronomers. Astronomy was often discussed at home especially since their mother often worked and hosted occasional meetings at their home in Diego, one of the numerous cities in the form of space stations orbiting Earth. Their parents had met in University whilst studying astronomy. It seemed logical that Xander and perhaps Jelina would follow in their footsteps. Maybe because he was the elder sibling, most of his friends and relatives had already assumed that it was him, not Jelina, who would pursue a career in the ever expanding field of astronomy. He believed that at this stage of his life that the chances were greater that the more reflective Jelina may be the one following in their parent's footsteps. It was just that she rarely spoke to anyone bar Arielle about her future plans.

One of Xander's maternal uncles was a very famous physician. He was highly gifted and perhaps could have been accomplished in many fields. He chose the practice of Medicine. He was younger than Xander and Jelina's mother and no doubt she was influenced by him and his accomplishments when she thought that Xander would make a great physician. The technology had advanced rapidly but she believed that Xander would have that unique combination of being able to utilize science and the human touch that made for the very best physicians. As logical and clinical as Xander was, he did have a very caring human side. One rarely saw this when he competed or participated in sporting events but it was quite obvious in his interactions with his sister, Jelina. Save for Dr Villanova and to certain extent Arielle, he understood her better than anyone else. They did share common chromosomes after all.

Xander often relived scenes from his memory. It was a trait of the Villanovas. Like now, when very quiet and undisturbed, he could almost experience the events, so vivid and lifelike they were. He could hear the actual voices if he closed his eyes and often had to remind himself that it was a memory, not a current occurrence. Just a shade off auditory hallucinations. At times like this he was not sure whether having such a vivid and brilliant memory was a blessing or curse. The mind would literally play tricks on him especially if he provided the necessary fuel. He wished that there was more to do during this leg of their trip.

VII.

The monotonous drone of the Pelican 25 was suddenly interrupted by a low hissing sound. This was quickly followed by three low pitch blasts that one could feel as well as hear, as they were in the lower frequency bands. Xander looked up surprised. The emergency lights came on and he quickly realized that he was indeed dealing with an emergent situation. It took him a fraction of a second to respond even though he had faced this exact scenario in simulations dozens of times before. He glanced over at the panels. All the instruments were active and fully engaged. He glanced over at his sister and friends. They were all sleeping peacefully and would not awaken unless he activated the reverse sequences.

The thought of radioing for help momentarily entered his mind. He quickly dismissed it. The first thing they would ask would be the information on his exact location, the position of the threat, their projected path, the actual chances of collision and other such data. He needed to determine those first. When he did, he could most likely take the needed course of action.

He was a bit surprised that his brow was moist despite the cool enclosure of the Pelican 25. He instinctively knew that there was only one type of emergency they could experience at this distance from the Sun whilst still in the system. The exact reason he was required to remain awake. Small icy fragments, most likely debris from comets, floated around in poorly defined orbits and could collide with passing ships. Even though the chances of a collision were very small, a few ships were known to be lost this way. They have almost always been ships that were on total autopilot at the time. Ship sensors did a great job of detecting these icy rocks but because of the speed of travel, there was usually just a small amount of time to alter course.

Xander looked over the instruments again. He could now visualize the rock that ship sensors detected in their path. The ship computers were working at optimal speed spitting out calculations and projections based on incoming real time data. It had just approximated the size of the rock. The ice rock was tiny relatively speaking. It was about sixty meters in diameter, just over half the length of a football field in width and thickness! He could not get a good read on the weight of this chunk of rock since the exact density was not known. It did not matter anyway. If the Pelican 25 were to hit an object of that size head on, it would be instantly reduced to fragments. The largest would probably be no larger than a golf ball.

Xander's clinical mind had kicked in and he was not overly anxious but he was on heightened alert. He was waiting for the instruments to project how close or rather how far they would pass by this uncharted icy rock. He knew that the first set of alarms was only triggered if they were going to be within 10,000 miles from a larger threatening body. Beyond that, he would not have been alerted of the potential threat and they would have sailed by unsuspecting. He was expecting a number somewhere between 1000 and 10,000 miles. If it were under 100 miles, the emergency sequences for waking up everyone would be automatically activated. All the ships power would then be diverted towards activating powerful magnetic shields to evade collision. It was an in built safety mechanism.

As he was awaiting the numbers, the second set of alarms came on. His heart skipped a beat. The alarms and instruments now indicated that they were going to pass within 1000 miles of the floating block of ice. *Trust my luck*, Xander thought. A rare phenomenon would happen on his very first trip piloting away from the system. Xander cursed under his breath. He was not given much to using his energy unproductively. He now had the choice of waking up the others or navigating by himself. He quickly figured that it would be too much risk to bring the others up in such a short space of time. He had no more than three minutes before they would pass or collide with this chunk of outer system debris. Xander wished his father was here. He almost always seemed to know what to do. He knew that the flight path of the Pelican 25 was being recorded and if the ship survived, a detailed log of all that took place would be available. Not so if they hit that opaque rock with little or no light reflecting from it.

Everything seemed to happen in slow motion. It seemed a long time since the first alarm went off and Xander was dreaming about seemingly mundane career choices. But it was less than two minutes ago. All the screens were flashing now. As they were getting closer, the calculations of how close they would pass from this nasty rock were getting more accurate. All Xander knew at the moment was that they were going to be within 1000 miles of it. Again, in a fleeting moment of panic, he thought of rousing the others. But he resisted. Wait for the next set of numbers. Surely he would have these in less than 30 seconds. The craft had dropped one notch in speed as was normal in these situations. It allowed more time to gauge the oncoming object. Xander stuck a hand out and dropped the speed of the craft another level. The computers responded instantly to his biometrics. They were in the middle of nowhere, on the outer verges of the system and they should be accelerating as they prepared to enter the pathways, not decelerating. Xander decided to trust his judgment. He knew that they had to hit the pathways at a certain critical speed for hyperspace travel. Otherwise it was a no go. He was hoping that after they passed the ice rock he would have enough time to get back up to optimal speed. He hoped.

Xander was not a person of inaction. He would make necessary decisions without second guessing. Even if they were life and death. He was confident and flexible enough as not to always go by the book. His willingness to manually override the speed of the Pelican 25 instead of allowing it to be adjusted by the computers proved just that. He would continue to be pro active. Too much was at stake. He involuntarily glanced over at his sister and friends sleeping. He performed his best under duress and in critical situations. It took a lot out of him but observers would never have guessed. He seemed to do it effortlessly yet nine of ten people would have not have downgraded their speed manually.

Xander was correct yet again. The extra time gained was invaluable. He had bought them more than 30 seconds. The computers were giving out more precise data. The rock was now measured at 62.5 metes in length 55 meters in width and it was 48 meters thick. *One of millions in the outer system that seemed to serve no purpose except to get in the way of travel,* Xander thought. Xander took a few deep breaths. Without planning to he again glanced over to his sister and friends. Sleeping like babies they were oblivious to anything that was going on around them and with him. The joys of anesthesia. He turned his head away with some effort back to the panels. He was the captain of this ship. It came with some responsibilities and he planned to shoulder them.

Xander would not have known it but if you were to have his heart rate monitored, it had gone up by 60%. His brow and face were wet now. His eyes were flitting from screen to screen. He was awaiting the single most important calculation which should be coming anytime soon. The exact distance that they would pass by this rock. Anything under 500 miles, he would have to alter course. This would necessitate fresh calculations with no guarantee that their flight path would be clear. In fact, there would be a statistically greater chance of running into debris as there would have been less time and planning to plot such a course compared to their original flight path.

"Come on, Come on," he urged the computers.

Each second seemed like an eternity as time seemed to have been suspended. And they were not at any time interfaces. They were still under the normal physical laws of the System.

He made no pretences of not talking aloud to himself anymore. For all practical purposes, he was alone.

"Come on baby, come on," he urged again. It was not a voice command to the computer but more like one urging one's favorite horse during a race. The machines were all working optimally. But they depended on the input of live data to make precise calculations and projections of bodies moving at this speed. It was like trying to calculate if two bullets with paths at right angles to each other would collide and if they were to miss by how far they would.

There were three sharps blasts that made Xander almost jump out of his skin. He could not tell instantly whether it was the next level of emergency or critical information notification. The longest fraction of a second he ever experienced passed as he stared at the screens, eyes wide open.

He let out a deep breath and exulted

"Oh yes."

"Oh YES," he reiterated.

A number had finally settled on the screens.

A beautiful number.

A comforting number.

Seven hundred and sixty eight and three tenths miles.

768.3 miles.

They were safe. No need to panic. No need to change course. It was not even as close as he thought when the second set of alarms went off. Sure it was less than 1000 miles. But 768.3 miles was a good number indeed.

Xander was breathing more steadily now. With little or no hesitation and even before passing the icy rock, he notched up their speed one level.

No time to waste. He was confident of his ship's computers and sensors. They need to get back to critical speed before entering the pathways. As soon as they passed this rock he would take it back up to their original speed.

Xander looked at the time. Less than 10 minutes before he activated the sequence for him to go under. The time had passed. Not the way he had initially hoped. Hyperspace travel was just around the bend.

The others were still sleeping peacefully. As innocent as ever.

He mopped his brow one last time. Took a few more deep breaths as he prepared for the Pathway travel.

PART 2
Aqualon

I.

Xander stirred first. He reflexly rubbed his eyes. An involuntary yawn and body stretching followed as if he was being roused from a deep sleep. Which was essentially what it was.

Mondeus awoke within the minute followed soon after by Jelina and then Arielle. It was no coincidence that the boys awoke first despite having had the same amount of anesthesia per unit body weight as the girls. Perhaps something to do with a hardwired evolutionary trait. Alertness and the protective instinct of guarding the tribe, that resided predominantly in the amydala, a tiny part of the brain.

They could all feel the pull of the rapidly decelerating spacecraft. It had only been a few minutes since they catapulted out of the Pathways traveling under physical laws and speeds that were unimaginable just eight hundred years ago. Everything went as planned during their trip through the Pathways. The instruments indicated that anyway. It seemed as if they were only asleep for a few hours. Xander noted from the instruments that he was under for 18 hours. The others for almost nineteen hours. Other than mild body aches and feeling lead-legged, there were little or no after effects of the Pathway travel.

The sequence of reawakening was automatically activated. It was based on numerous factors including the pressure outside the spacecraft and the decelerating forces that came into play when a nearby star was detected. In a few minutes they would be under the pull of the double suns or binary stars of the Ixodia system. As their speeds dropped below a certain point, it was safe to be awake and be under normal environmental conditions again. The rules of travel were now just as in their home system with a few differences given the fact that only one planet orbited these suns.

"I feel as if I drank cheap wine," groaned Arielle.

"My head hurts too," mumbled Jelina.

"Just a little hangover from the sedation," offered Mondeus.

"I know, I know," they both chimed.

They were all getting more alert by the second.

"Xander, are you sure that you put us to sleep in hyperspace?" Arielle teased.

Xander already knew that Arielle was feeling better based on that question.

He didn't answer. Jelina noted that Xander hadn't said anything since he awoke. She sensed that all did not go well when he was awake prior to the Pathway travels. She would ask later. Not now. No need to alarm the others.

Xander's mind had drifted back to the alarm and near panic of the possible collision with the icy rock. It seemed so far way away now. And indeed it was. He shook his head as he tried to shrug off the memory. He would tell them later. For now, it was time to concentrate on piloting the ship to a safe landing on their vacation site.

Mondeus and Jelina also scanned the panel and instruments. They were dead on course. "Looks like we have a couple of hours until we get to Aqualon," Xander announced.

"Enough time to relax and prepare for the beaches and the real vacation," he added.

That lifted everyone.

"Captain Xander, permission to watch TV?" Arielle asked.

"Sure."

They were now in a populated system. The choices were many. Arielle flipped around the channels. Numerous advertisements for the various moons on which to spend your time and accumulated credits! And what beautiful sceneries displayed. Forested areas. Beaches. Waterfalls. It seemed as if they had it all here. No wonder this was one of the more popular vacation spots in this part of the traveled galaxy.

Mondeus preferred to use his headphones and listen to the newsflashes. Taking in current events. A new governor on one of Ixodia's populated moons. Some unexplained signals picked up from a remote part of the galaxy. Another giant space station completed ahead of schedule. Nothing too much out of the ordinary. More ads on the screen that Arielle was looking at. Places for couples only. Tours of some of the uninhabited moons. They had already decided prior to departure from their system which moons they were going to visit. Too late for the ads now.

Jelina decided to go to her room and freshen up. Xander made some final adjustments to the ship computers and then also departed to his quarters.

Mondeus in the meantime was fidgety.

"Aren't you tired of watching the same ads over and over?" he asked Arielle.

She didn't answer. A hair product ad was now on the screen. It was one that Arielle had used before. She had liked it. Her long brown hair did need extra attention and she did not mind. Plus Xander had hinted that he liked her long hair.

Mondeus and Arielle were alone in the main cabin area. Mondeus tried again, "Don't you think that those could wait until we get on land?"

He was looking to provoke an answer and even though Arielle had planned to ignore him, a reply slipped from her mouth.

"What's the rush Isaac?"

Mondeus's face became a bit flushed and Arielle immediately regretted the comment. She liked him like a little brother but he could be annoying at times. Xander, Jelina and her had agreed before this trip began, that they would ignore his remarks if they were not courteous. There was a simple reason for that. Even though Mondeus could be the nicest person you'd ever meet, he did not tolerate being off solid ground for any length of time well. Added to that, they were in a small confined space. In trips that were hardly any inconvenience to a Voyager or even a Lunite, Mondeus would get progressively restless. He was an Original, after all and was accustomed to a lot of solid ground and expansive land space. It was likely that this occurred beyond his level of consciousness. Sort of a perpetual "cabin fever" for him.

"Isaac huh?" he retorted with flashing eyes and a piercing stare at Arielle.

Arielle chose not to say anything. She knew that as quickly as Mondeus became testy he would revert to being his usual jovial self but she should not have called him "Isaac."

Isaac was not really Mondeus's middle name but a nickname. His full name was Mondeus Rohan Ventori. He was born in the region of what was originally the South American country of the Guyanas, just north of the equator. His school zone for the gifted fell under the Plato system of schools. The catchments area was between the equator and the 20th parallel. And it was at the Plato schools he first crossed paths with Arielle, Jelina and Xander.

Isaac was a nickname that he earned in school a few years ago. It was both complimentary and at times used to tease the boy genius. It arose when Mondeus disputed one of the teachings of the great Isaac Newton. Even though his teachers vehemently disagreed with him, they subsequently accepted his view as an alternative way of expressing one of Newton's numerous theories. When Arielle called him Isaac a few moments ago the implication was clear. She was responding to his needling with one of her own. It was probably not the best time for him to be called Isaac. *But still, boy geniuses need to learn to live and share with others,* Arielle thought. He could not always do as he felt living in a society with norms and laws even if he did not believe that they applied to him. No doubt he would get better as he got older and more experienced. And he was learning from Xander with each passing day. This trip was good for Mondeus in more ways than one.

II.

The teenagers all gathered in the main cabin to get a good look at the Ixodia system. They did have a bit of free time before they docked at Aqualon. They could afford to pass it in idle conversation and anticipation of exploring this system.

"We have to decide by tomorrow on which day we will go to the uninhabited moon," Xander said.

"Why?" asked Arielle. "I thought that our travel plans were pretty fixed."

"We have two windows for short trips to it," Mondeus said.

Both Jelina and Xander nodded.

"We will be on Aqualon for about three weeks of Earth's time. Since the days on Aqualon are about thirty hours long, we effectively have about 17 days of vacation here. The uninhabited moon, Riad, will orbit closest to us on Day # 3 and Day # 14. We can skip over on these days most efficiently," Xander explained.

"We had originally thought of going over later in our vacation," he continued. "But Jelina had suggested to me that we may be tired and have less energy by then."

"Let's go soon," Arielle said wistfully. Mondeus was quiet.

"I guess we will have to vote on it," Xander replied.

"All in favor of an early trip to Riad?" Xander asked.

Arielle and Jelina raised their hands. After a few seconds Mondeus did too.

No point in asking for those against it. Xander would have chosen the latter date but he would go along with the majority. There was not much else to decide one way or the other.

"Ok then, it's settled," Xander said. "We will go to Riad on Day # 3."

The sunlight was very bright. They had all the windows on transparent settings. Seeing the two Suns side by side was very picturesque and they could now clearly see Ixodia and its orbiting moons. They were all different shades from green to white. The teenagers were quiet for a while as they took in this unusual scenery.

The Ixodia system was relatively unique. Ixodia was a large Jupiter sized Goldilocks planet. It was the only planet in this system orbiting the two Suns. The unique feature of Ixodia was that it had 147 moons orbiting it. They were at a distance and temperature range that allowed relatively easy conversion for them, to be habitable by humans. Some did not initially have the ideal balance of environmental gases, but these were adjusted by the complex systems that humans had developed. This had allowed humans to escape from the large bubbles that characterized early Lunar civilizations to a non-edificial way of life, aided by a man-made partial atmosphere.

Most of Ixodia's moons were inhabited with few exceptions. Even those that were uninhabited by humans had some animal and plant life. One could safely live there for weeks if desired. Because of the existence of water in all three states on many of the moons, an abundance of beaches, tropical type forests and very lush plant life, these moons had become coveted vacation spots in the last century or so. Some of the other moons like Riad, were common destinations for camping and exploration.

Aqualon was the moon chosen by Xander and his classmates to spend their time between School year 15 A and 15 B. It was one of the larger moons of Ixodia and its main attraction was its large number of tranquil and colorful beaches. Its name reflected that. Because of the binary Suns, the water on this moon was almost always warm. The mineral deposits indigenous to Aqualon shaded the shallow seas to every possible color imaginable. The size of this particular moon allowed it to have many hills and even a few small mountains. With lush tropical type forests and a smattering of waterfalls it had more variety than most of the other moons. No wonder it was extremely popular amongst teenagers and young college students. It was as close to paradise as one could imagine. Added to this, it was in the Milky Way at just over a hundred light years away. With several known Pathways to this system, it was relatively easy to travel to and thousands headed this way at every school break. Xander,

Jelina, Arielle and Mondeus had heard first hand the enjoyable tales of returning visitors and could barely wait their turn to visit. Their parents had agreed to this trip if they had excelled at the Plato school. That, each one of them had done!

III.

The traffic was nowhere as dense as Earth or Central Station back in the System. However there were quite a few crafts around. The major difference was most of these crafts were smaller as opposed to the giants that were used for transportation in the System. There were quite a few Pelican 25's around. This allowed them to dock at small hangars. In fact, Xander was going to dock at a station that was merely 10 miles from the beach house that they had booked. The hangar was a bit inland—but this was to be expected as no one wanted to utilize precious beachside real estate for spaceports and hangars.

"I can already see the hills on Aqualon," the effervescent Arielle piped up.

"If you were on this side you could see the green waters and beaches too," Jelina chimed in.

As always Xander brought their thoughts back to the present with his practical words.

"We will land in about 15 minutes," he said.

Arielle was busy contemplating which bikini to wear first on the beach.

Mondeus was preoccupied with something in the corner of the main cabin but was apparently listening.

"We are a stone's throw away," he said to Xander. Implying, of course, that they would land very soon on Aqualon. Since they were no longer in

Deep Space neither Xander nor Mondeus had a chance of throwing a stone that far. It was a small hangar, so it would be unlikely that there was a wait time to land.

"We will have to hover," Xander said. The thought crossed Mondeus's mind and as he was just about to ask "Why?" when he realized the answer.

He was a tad annoyed because he had not fully done his homework. Pretty much it meant that the landing area was hilly and they would have to hover over the hangar for a short while and then descend vertically instead of a runway type landing. The Pelican 25 was designed for either.

"We are close to maximum weight so we have to be careful," added Xander.

Xander was always meticulous and careful when he did not need to say anything to reassure the others. The risky part of their travel was well behind them. They were on the high side on weight because they were loaded with supplies. At the last minute they decided to carry their own hovercraft for ground transport instead of loaning one. It was one of those ultra lightweight models and it would save them on cost leaving their credits to buy more important things like exotic gemstones! The hovercraft was stored in the underbelly of the ship. In addition to the usual supplies, they also had Mondeus's ever reliable robot, Tytum, with them. Mondeus had wanted to bring his other robot too, but Xander's father had recommended that they make do with one shared robot. This would aid in keeping their cargo weight down.

The Pelican 25 systems had already locked into that of the grounded spaceport that doubled as a hangar. They were flying at low speed and low altitude and could see most of Aqualon unaided by telescopic settings of the portholes of the ship. Everyone was excited but Xander remained stoically at the controls. Most of the landing was automated as the ship received guided signals from the spaceport.

"Can we hit the beaches today Captain Xander?" Arielle asked half serious about it. Jelina also looked on eagerly for an answer.

"I think there is enough daylight left since the days here are a bit longer," Jelina offered.

Xander was measured in his response but optimistic by his standards.

"It depends on how quickly we unload and get to the house. If there are still a couple hours of daylight, I don't see any reason why we shouldn't."

"We could go in the night," Mondeus suggested, just in case they were a bit slow in disembarking and carrying supplies from the ship to the house. Mondeus was not known to be the most physical worker of the group. Sure he was a bit younger than the rest but he had programmed his robot at home to do as many manual tasks as possible. No wonder he wanted to bring it with him.

"We could go in the night only for an hour or two after sunset," Xander said.

"Skinny dipping isn't too much fun after that."

Arielle's eyes twinkled mischievously. Both she and Jelina knew what Xander meant. The water temperature on Aqualon dropped after sunset. The seas were relatively shallow and for a couple of hours the temperature was still tolerable. After that it became much cooler.

"We could go directly to the house and return for the supplies tomorrow." Mondeus took one last try at immediate gratification but in the process made his aversion for work much more apparent. Xander didn't even answer this time. He looked at Mondeus and his answer was clear. They were going to unload their supplies before they headed to any beach. Mondeus let out a short sigh. He did try.

The Pelican 25 was at a standstill now. It was hovering a few thousand feet over the spaceport, landing gear out. It readjusted its position slightly making it exactly in line with the spot on the port that it was going to take. These crafts could land in a space that was no larger than a couple meters of their actual size. The port seemed pretty empty and no other craft was descending right now. Lots of available space. The Pelican 25 descended slowly down on the landing area. It slowed even more as it neared the ground. Landing gear extended, it almost stopped before it touched the ground. And then it touched down with nary a shudder. The shock absorbers of the landing gear took most of the credit for that. All the teenagers including Xander clapped briefly.

"We're here! Yay!" they exclaimed.

Xander quickly extruded the wheels and they motored the short distance to their designated hangar, where the Pelican 25 would remain, except for their brief trip to Riad. Tired but excited they began to unload. Even Mondeus seemed energized now that there was an immediate reward in sight.

IV.

It took them more than an hour before they unloaded most of their stuff and packed it into the Maglev type hovercraft.

"This is the worst part of any vacation," Mondeus said as he huffed and puffed. The others did not disagree with him. Still when things needed to be done, it needed to be done and done well. There was no way they were going to do a slip slop job under Xander's watch.

The hovercraft had four seats and a lot of cargo room which was virtually full now. This was after leaving some non essential supplies in the ship. The seats were arranged in two rows and without asking Mondeus jumped into the front row next to the driver's controls.

"So where do we put Tytum?" Jelina asked.

"He can sit in the back next to the cargo," Xander suggested.

"Perhaps Mondeus can sit near his friend," Arielle offered, hoping that she could share the front row with Xander whilst Mondeus sat next to the Titanium alloyed robot.

Mondeus muttered something unintelligible under his breath. He loved his robots but wanted the unimpeded view from the front row of the hovercraft and would not budge that easily.

Arielle sighed. A knowing sigh of acceptance. Mondeus couldn't take a hint. Maybe she would have to break her promise and return to bribing him with milk chocolate once more. She had only desisted when they noted that Mondeus had gone 10 centiles beyond his ideal body weight.

"It's OK Arielle, we'll be just fine like this," Jelina said. "The ride is just under 10 minutes anyway and we will be there before you know it."

"All right, but it is quite a scenic view," she conceded. "According to the travel clips, there is a hill first, two small mountains and a ravine to cross. Should be fun."

"Buckle up," Xander said as they were about to embark.

"We will be traveling at more than 100 mph."

With the press of a button the seatbelts slid into place and were locked allowing Xander to take off at a surprisingly quick acceleration.

They had kept the top of the hovercraft down and the aromatic wind hit their faces sending a thrill through them all. This is what vacations were for. You could feel it, smell it and soon would be able to taste it when they hit the salty air of Aqualon beaches. They glided up the first hill with such ease that they could have been on flat land and wouldn't have known any different. The down slope was even more fun. Everyone was taking in the lush green around them. Multicolored flowers dotted the scenery. The variety of trees and vegetation was impressive to even Mondeus who was an Original. To the Voyagers and Lunite it was breathtaking. As they gained elevation on the first mountain slope it looked even more spectacular. There were small clouds floating in the valley and some mist even at this time of the day. As they climbed higher, they saw a sight that none of them had witnessed before. *Four* rainbows.

Not one or two, but four. At the same time. The two suns of Ixodia had combined to work their magic. It seemed as if they could almost reach out and touch them, so close they were. An optical illusion it was, and difficult to believe!

The Hovercraft rode about one foot above six inch wide rails that provided levitation. They had reached the top of the first mountain and were descending into the ravine between the two mountains. There was a small river between these two and the rails were elevated for several hundred feet. This was not uncommon in territories where it rained a lot. These rivers and creeks formed out of the necessity to drain the rainy areas. Xander was initially engrossed in the scenery as they all were but he looked up from time to time. He blinked and looked again. There was a section of rail missing at the bottom of the mountain. *Completely missing.* It seemed as if the heavy rains had washed away parts of the foundation that supported this piece of rail. And it had collapsed.

"Look!" Xander gasped.

They all looked ahead and saw it too. It was quite close and there was no way that they could stop in time. If the hovercraft did not get any Maglev support for a couple hundred feet, it would go careening into mountainside. Worse yet, into the rocks laid bare by centuries of the flowing river. Mondeus gaped. Arielle and Jelina froze. They barely had enough time to comprehend their situation much less react to it. How could no one have reported this break in the line? It must have happened very recently. The perils of using the path less traveled!

Xander seemed to react in slow motion. He knew they had only a few seconds before they reached the break in the rail. A thought surfaced in his head even as he tried to assess their predicament.

"Why did stuff like this always happen to them?"

When he had recounted their travels to his friends, they often enviously said "I wish we had adventures like those."

What they did not know was, at the time those adventures were taking place, how much they wished it was not happening. Xander recognized that they had two choices that did not include crashing into the mountainside. They either tried to stop the vehicle—which in his estimation was close to impossible given their current speed and proximity to the break in the tracks. Or they did nothing and hoped that the speed and momentum of the craft would take them over the couple hundred feet of missing line and reestablish connection with the unaffected rail. Whether due to a moment of inaction or not—he chose the latter.

There was not time for consultation of the others. Mondeus wondered why he did not try stopping but this was no time to object. Arielle wondered if he was crazy as he actually increased their speed. In the split second that he was doing this, Jelina realized what he was planning. The faster speed would propel them further along the missing line and increase their chance of vaulting the missing rail. Still it was difficult to calculate how good their chances were. As they got closer, they saw that the piece of missing rail was longer than they initially thought. They held their collective breaths as they approached the gap. They were going very fast now. Utilizing the maximum speed of the hovercraft plus the momentum gained by going downhill on the mountainous slope. As they were about to hit the broken line, Xander yanked the controls and tilted the craft upwards. *This may yet buy us a split second,* Xander thought. They moved over the ravine in slow motion. It looked first as if they were going to make it. But no, they were *not* going to make it!

They were a few feet short and the craft now came under gravity losing most of its forward propulsion. They were so close now but were dropping downwards into the ravine and the river four hundred feet below.

The craft shuddered. Then it shuddered again. It miraculously stopped dropping and it was at a standstill for a full second. Somehow it seemed to latch on to the pull at the end of the rail. It captured the rail and started moving forward again. Quickly back on the tracks. More precisely suspended at about 12 inches above the tracks. Moving uphill again.

"My goodness, that was really close," Arielle found her voice first.

"For a moment, I didn't think we were going make it," Jelina said.

"It's OK now," Xander said quietly.

Mondeus was still wiping his brow, and feeling his heart thumping in his chest, having not yet recovered his voice.

V.

The sun was setting. It was still quite warm. The beach was sparsely populated at this time as many tourists had gone in for the day. Xander, Jelina and Arielle were already in the water, waist deep. Mondeus was sitting on a large rock at the edge of the beach watching the gulls go by.

They had gotten to the beach house without any further mishaps. They unpacked only a portion of their belongings and hurried off to make use of the remaining sunlight. The rays were still strong, despite both suns being low in the sky. It was good to feel the solid ground under their feet again after a relatively long trip.

Mondeus was pensive and seemed a bit lost sitting in his over sized swimming trunks on a beach on Aqualon in the Ixodia system. A very long way from his childhood home in South America.

Mondeus Rohan Ventori was from a large family. He was one of five children born to his parents, in a small farming town in the Guyanas. Fourth in a family of three girls and two boys. He was very close to his family in some ways and in others he was not. He loved them dearly. Yet, at times he found it difficult to communicate with them. They just did not understand his ideas. They knew he was different but that did not make it any easier. His aunts and uncles and cousins all knew he was different. Exactly how, they were not sure.

Sure, he excelled at school but that was not all of it. He often had strange ideas. They all had stories from his early childhood of the things he did that were unexpected or not normal for kids of his age. He was bored for the most part at school but could not tell that to his parents. They placed a lot of effort and value on his education. To tell that to them would sink their hearts and he could not bear that so he pretended to be interested. All his siblings did well at school and as such it was easier to hide behind them in a pack.

He concocted imaginary games and played them in his head. He made up and modified well established theories. Most of these he soon forgot as he had little evidence to support them and they were based on his fancy at the time. Sometimes they returned to him in a couple of years. Mondeus did not know that the stuff that went on in his head was not the norm for most kids. How could he? He was only a tween who could be easily ignored by adults who had no clue about what he was thinking. It was more comfortable for them.

Mondeus learnt to spend time by himself at an early age. It allowed him to think and drift. It was peaceful and he could travel to imaginary places.

He did choose some odd times for these reveries, for sure. Still, these became accepted by his immediate family as just being Mondeus. He loved when they call him Mondy and wish he could share everything with them. But how could he?

Such was the price of genius. More pains than glory. He had learnt to live with it. Deep down he was an optimist and always believed that where there is a will there was a way. He hoped that he would get a chance to meet other people like him, crazy ideas and all. He intuitively knew that there was more out there that he was experiencing now. And that he was rapidly outgrowing his native little town.

His break came unexpectedly one day in form of a communication from school. Mondeus had done an aptitude test at school. He did not think it was important and did not even mention it to his parents. When his results were compared to his peers at school, he was well beyond the 99th centile. That attracted the attention of the school principal. It was the best score ever documented for his school. The principal recommended a special school for Mondeus. One that would be better suited to his gifts and talents. Not only would the Plato system of schools accept him but they would place him in a grade one year higher than the norm for his age.

Mondeus was elated and sad at the same time. It meant that he would have to leave home. It was not an easy decision. Initially his parents did not think that someone his age should go to school 800 miles away from home. Eventually they gave in, knowing that it was best for Mondy. They were astute enough to realize that Mondeus had special needs. And these would not be met in this small town. As Mondeus got older, he realized that his parents knew much more about him than he gave them credit for, even if they did not comprehend his actual ideas.

It was after leaving home and going to the Plato schools that he met Xander, Jelina and Arielle for the first time. His best friends. They accepted his ways and understood his solitude at times. Even his brooding. That is why they did not insist that he went into the water with them. They knew he would, in his own time.

A gull passed so close to Mondeus that he felt the draft from its wings. *Good thing it did not make a deposit on me,* he thought. This was followed by a large flock, flying very low. Mondeus noted all of this without appearing to. It was almost as if he had a subconscious log. Events took place while he was thinking but his thoughts were reality to him at the time and the events registered as fleeting thoughts. Mondeus was peaceful. He was happy. He loved open spaces.

Looking up, the shallow sea with aquamarine waters stretched for miles. All the way to the horizon. It had an inexplicable calming effect on him. Perhaps some vestige of human evolution.

VI.

"Wake up sleepy head," Xander urged.

Mondeus groaned and muttered something and rolled over.

"Come on," Xander insisted. "The girls have been up for more than an hour."

"Okay," Mondeus responded sluggishly, still unable to drag himself out of bed.

He felt as if they were still on the Pelican 25 with artificially induced light-dark cycles but they were not. It was the first morning in that beautiful house on the beach on Aqualon. Both suns were already high in the sky. They allowed themselves to sleep as long as they wished and it had been almost 13 hours since they went to bed. No problem there as with the long days, there was lots of time to relax and do nothing. Yet,

Mondeus always seemed to be the last to get out of bed unless they were on the verge of a big event.

Xander pulled the drapes and the bright light surprised Mondeus. *That is what you get for two suns,* Mondeus thought. It was only mid morning but the light seemed almost as if it were midday. Mondeus was awake now. He looked out of the windows still lying in his bed.

What a beautiful sight!

A wide expanse of beach. Stretching for miles in either direction. Light brown sand that changed into lighter brown and then tan as it approached the water. Closer to the water the sand became white as it disappeared under the water. A seamless transition. They were less than 50 meters from the water. It lapped playfully on the beach with the smallest of waves that grew out of tiny ripples. And yet, at times it was still, waiting to be disturbed.

It was not bare either. In fact, there was a lot of greenery around. Probably a testament to the frequent rainfall. There were numerous palm trees on either side of the cabins. Some were actually on the beach and not very far from the water. In the area of the light brown sand they ventured, but not quite into the white sands. They had various sizes of fruit. Maybe some were edible. They were not sure. They would ask. One type was very similar to coconut palms that were native to Mondeus's part of Earth. Another had much smaller marble sized fruit that grew in bunches as well. The fruit seemed to change from a lighter green to a darker green and then brownish yellow as they got riper.

And then the water. As you lifted your eyes, you saw the water.

Aquamarine.

No, it was green.

No, it was blue.

No, it was changing its color. With lighter and darker shades.

Chameleonic in nature.

How could that be?

Xander saw it too but needed no explanation. It seemed strange but beautiful. They did not notice it the night before. Mondeus wanted to ask but he was already moving towards the verandah on the cabin, where he could have an unobstructed view of the sea. Xander was there earlier.

"The water is changing color," Mondeus commented without asking why.

"It does seem so, doesn't it," Jelina and Arielle chorused from the kitchenette. The girls had just returned after acquiring a wide variety of fresh fruits, some of which were native only to the Ixodia system. As far as they knew anyway. There was no rush to have breakfast as they were not on schedule anymore. But they were now starving.

It took Mondeus only a few seconds on the verandah to understand why the water changed colors. There were many clouds moving about in the sky. There were blue patches of sky that were quickly decorated as clouds of uneven density floated in. These cast variable shadows on the water, making it appear to change colors. The effect was obviously magnified by the presence of two suns. Because the sun was low in the sky then, they did not notice it the previous evening. *Hmmm,* Mondeus thought, *there is a logical explanation for it.* This comforted him.

"Breakfast is ready," announced Jelina smilingly

"And you guys, don't get too comfortable and expect to get served," Jelina added. And for good measure. "Tomorrow is your turn."

"And we will all live to regret it," Arielle interjected, directing her comments more to Mondeus than Xander.

She could guess how this would play out. As it usually did. Xander would help to get meals ready. He was very capable. Mondeus would make some nondescript excuse and he would offer to do the dishes and tidy up instead. He would then program, Tytum, the robot to do the work. And then reason that he had done his share. She and Jelina would offer to help Xander and they were back to square one. Actually they did not mind much as they were on vacation and could do everything at their own pace.

They sat in the main room of the cozy beach house with glass windows on three sides. The table was smallish but very adequate for four. They all had a very good view of the beach and sea. Having breakfast and listening to the sound of the water with occasional waves. The feel of the slightly warm wind coming through open doors on their skin. There was nothing like being on vacation on the beaches of Aqualon. It was Paradise indeed.

Going to the beach twice a day. Stretching out under the suns. Retuning to the cabin and lazing. Watching movies. Eating out at the nearby restaurants. Eating in. One could get used to this. School already seemed to be far far away. As a matter of fact, it was.

It was in an entirely different system.

VII.

"We're leaving tomorrow for Riad," Jelina complained. "It seems as if we just got here."

"Actually, we just got here two days ago," Arielle reminded her.

"Maybe, we should have made our plans to visit Riad at the second pass," Jelina added. "It's so nice here."

"I could live here forever," Arielle agreed.

"You think you could but after a few weeks you would get bored and want to return to our home System," the cerebral Jelina pointed out.

"I guess so, but right now I don't feel that way," Arielle persisted.

"We'll have fun on Riad," Jelina said encouragingly.

"Do you think we will have adventures on Riad?" Arielle asked wistfully.

"If you call sleeping in caves an adventure, we surely will. Other than that the moon is uninhabited. Doesn't leave much room for adventures, does it?"

"I guess not," Arielle sighed.

Voices came from the kitchen that reached the girls. Xander had gone to the town to get some fresh food and supplies in preparation for their trip to Riad.

Mondeus was in the kitchen alone. That is if you considered him in the presence of Tytum alone.

Mondeus was at it again. They heard him saying.

"Excellent."

"Excellent!"

Time and again.

He was programming Tytum to do all the household chores.

It was his way of reinforcing the desired behavior.

"Excellent!"

Sometimes the teenagers wondered if it was not easier for him to just do the tasks himself. They would. They imagined that Mondeus got some pleasure by getting Tytum to function in new environments and learn new tasks.

As expected, he had volunteered to do the cleaning and tidying. That included washing dishes after meals. They let him be. Now it was him and Tytum.

Tytum was a lightweight titanium robot that Mondeus kept with him at his quarters at school. It was almost like a friend to him. Tytum was not quite an Android but a complicated highly functional mobile robot. Mondeus constantly upgraded its programs to do almost anything he wanted including getting stuff for him. If Mondeus wanted a glass of water, he would ask Tytum to get it for him. Tytum was quite competent but it took some time to get it to function well in a new environment. That is why Mondeus had to adjust its programs and reinforce its behavior in this new vacation house. It did have some equipment that was different from that of his earthly quarters. Not to mention that the dimensions of the rooms and hallways were different in this house. Notwithstanding it numerous sensors, Tytum had been known to bump into walls. It learnt quickly though. After its programs has been reinforced it made very few mistakes. Getting it to learn was obviously the challenge. Mondeus, as expected, rose to the challenge. It was time consuming but Mondeus did not seem to mind. If he had all the materials at his disposal, Mondeus would have made Tytum more Android-like. Perhaps one day he could still do this.

Tytum also had basic voice skills. It would answer with short words including "Yes", "No", "Affirmative", "Negative" and the other slang that Mondeus programmed like "Way to go", "Yahoo", "Got it" etc. It was not advanced enough to respond to conversations. It was voice activated and tone specific so Mondeus could issue instructions from across the room. After some compromise, he had set it to accept instructions from Xander as well.

The girls did not care too much for Tytum and usually stayed out of its way.

They knew that Tytum was like a big toy to Mondeus. Yet it had its uses.

It could be set in a guard mode, whereby it could provide security. It would detect intrusions by any humans it did not identify and sound an alarm. Or it would inform or warn them depending on the mode it was set to in the particular situation. This came in handy when they went camping or stayed in relatively desolate places.

Once at school, Mondeus had forgotten to reset Tytum and it was left in the high security mode. Someone's pet cat had come into the room and Tytum responded by creating a raucous uproar. Mondeus almost lost his privileges to keep Tytum at school. He managed to hold on to him after many assurances that there would be no further public disturbances from Tytum. Mondeus seemed to forget at times that a simple power switch could put Tytum in an off mode.

"Excellent," Mondeus said, once again.

"No way," Tytum voiced.

"Way," said Mondeus.

Tytum was very much in the on mode now as it scurried back and forth stacking clean dishes neatly on the table counter.

VIII.

"Vacations are not for rushing," groaned Arielle as she finally settled in her seat of the Pelican 25 for their short trip to Riad.

"It is just the way the orbits are," Xander reminded her patiently.

"It would have been ideal to spend half our time on Aqualon and then the other half on Riad and then go home. But midway through our vacation Riad would be some distance away from Aqualon. Not much we can do about it."

"Yes, yes," Arielle sighed.

"Maybe we should've gone to another moon." Arielle had to get one final protest in. Xander wisely did not respond. He did not think she was actually looking for an answer. As a matter of fact, they had looked into that scenario and came to the conclusion that Riad was a good choice for a few days of camping.

"You're just too lazy to move," Mondeus added. He thought that he knew the exact reason for Arielle's reluctance to leave Aqualon at this time. And Mondeus was not known for his diplomatic skills.

"I thought you were the one who needed a robot to do your chores," she responded.

Actually, they had been having a great time on Aqualon. They would return after a few days on Riad to continue the latter half of their vacation anyway.

"We will be back in a few days," Jelina tried to appease her.

"Can't wait," Arielle said with a tad of sarcasm.

"You didn't need to pack so much of your stuff," Mondeus interjected, as if to indicate less packing would be less of a bother.

"And the only thing you took was that titanium skeleton of a robot," retorted Arielle. "How much use is that going to be to us?"

"I am not leaving him behind," Mondeus said defensively. "He can help us do stuff."

Mondeus had decided to take Tytum despite the protests of the others.

Arielle knew that she had hit a touchy spot and decided that a subject change was in order. Jelina bailed her out.

"Anyone looking forward to the underground rivers as much as I am?" she asked. They all smiled. They knew that they could always count on Jelina to diffuse any situation.

They were airborne again aboard the Pelican 25. Xander was busy keying their coordinates for the relatively short trip to the uninhabited moon. Traveling from moon to moon in the Ixodia System was fairly easy and there was no need to stop at Ixodia's central station. In fact, the traffic to the uninhabited moons was very light. Only passing and first time visitors to the system made brief stops on some of them. Some were still not habitable for humans. Others were made so, using ultra modern techniques that produced habitable gas mixtures and raised oxygen levels.

Xander stepped away from the controls.

"We'd be there before you know it. No fights until we get there because I don't have much time for refereeing," he joked looking in the direction of Mondeus and Arielle.

"OK," Mondeus said "I'll leave him on board when we go camping."

Mondeus was still not quite ready to leave the Tytum discussion altogether. He referred to Tytum as a "he" while the others called the robot an "it". That just about summed it up.

Arielle glanced mischievously at him. Her twinkling eyes indicated that she was done fighting with Mondeus. She was older after all. Not to mention that Xander had seated himself just next to her. That always got her attention. She admired him and liked him very much. Sometimes she wondered what it would be like to have an older brother. One thing she was certain about—if she had a brother, she would like him to be like Xander. As much as possible.

Xander liked her too. In the beginning, he always thought of her as his sister's friend. More recently he could not help noticing how she dressed, how she kept her hair and the look she sometimes gave him. Most of all, this strange feeling just below his chest, he had told no one about. All of this was not lost on Jelina. She noticed it too and did not have to ask Xander about it. She sensed that Arielle and Xander were beginning to share a few things on a different dimension. They had also begun to communicate more non-verbally in recent times.

Not very long ago, the thought had crossed her mind, that if Xander and Arielle got closer, would she be left out? She knew her brother too well to entertain that as more than a passing thought. Still, she was subject to common and normal human emotions. They had shared too much in the past and she would always be special to him as he was to her. Since her mother went missing, they had become even closer as a family—if that were at all possible. She smiled to herself. She did not really mind Xander sitting next to Arielle. It made them all happy.

"Would you like me to get you a drink?" Arielle asked Xander politely.

"I will grab some fruit juice," Xander offered, getting up.

"It's beautiful in this system," Arielle continued on his return.

"I wish we could go to school here."

"It is beautiful indeed with so much of nature unspoiled," Xander agreed.

"But there are no natives of this system, so there are not many schools. Only a few for the family members of the people who work here. Not to mention you would miss your family if you stayed this far away from home."

One of Xander's few flaws, he had a way of injecting too much reality into the conversation. He was correct, of course. Yet, it was not in keeping with the setting of their present trip and Arielle's mood. They could see almost a dozen moons with the naked eye out of the windows of the Pelican 25. From a distance, the forested ones looked much prettier than the ones with less greenery. Yet, these were beautiful in their own unique way. Picturesque, with hills, mountains and craters. From space every contour and outline seemed to merge perfectly into another. The two suns cast shadows with varying degrees of light on the far sides of the moon. Some had large penumbras with only small areas of total darkness.

Riad would soon come into view with the naked eye. Based on its current location it only got dark for about one-third of its day. This was not a bad thing as it would allow them to get into some kind of sleep cycle. And should not be too demanding for their pineal glands and hormone secretion patterns.

Mondeus and Arielle were secretly hoping that there would be some adventures on Riad. Xander and Jelina were unimpressed with the possibilities of adventures on Riad. There did not seem to be too many on an uninhabited moon with no permanent settlement and hardly any animal life. Time would tell. So far, their trip had been anything but uneventful. Perhaps Riad too, may not be as mundane as they thought.

PART 3

Riad

I.

The four of them huddled around the campfire. It was cool but not cold. They were in an enormous cave with a dome shaped roof the size of a football field. A small stream flowed in one corner of the massive cave that was set at the base of a rocky hill. It was really an underground river that occasionally flooded the floor of the cave, when it rained heavily. There was no rain in the forecast for the next several days on Riad. Xander had gleamed that much environmental data from the ship's computer, prior to landing.

"Can you move over a bit?" Mondeus muttered.

He was sitting next to Arielle and thought that she was squashing him.

"You have lots of room," Arielle complained.

She had moved over to sit closer to Xander and Jelina. Mondeus was in the middle. And, of course, he complained of not having enough space.

"All right, you two, don't spoil the peace." Jelina reminded them.

"Maybe it's time for phantom stories?" Xander nudged. That got their attention and Mondeus quickly forgot that he was sitting between Xander and Arielle.

They had landed on Riad early that afternoon. Determined not to waste a single night of their vacation, they had decided to go camping on that first night. Jelina and Xander had mapped out possible sites earlier. They had settled on this large cave which was located fairly close to the Pelican 25 landing site.

It was even more magnificent than they imagined. They decided to dispense with artificial lights after it got dark and started a campfire with wood they had gathered. The aroma of roasted nuts floated through their nostrils. They bought these particular types of nuts on Aqualon for this specific purpose. They were similar to chestnuts that Mondeus was familiar with on Earth but this nut, native only to this part of the Ixodia system was called Wiffle nuts.

"Are we going to do ghost stories?" Mondeus prompted.

"Go right ahead," Jelina said.

"I don't know any new ones" Mondeus continued "And the good ones I know, you've already heard"

"Your turn then," Jelina indicated to Arielle.

"No, I'm afraid I'll scare Mondeus" Arielle mocked, covering her eyes.

"We all know that there are no ghosts and monsters," Mondeus said trying to be firm and logical. He didn't sound as convincing here in the desolate cave as he would have in his classroom at school.

He looked over at Xander. Xander was busy turning the Wiffle nuts in the fire. Jelina also was helping by tasting a smaller nut that was almost cooked.

"Mmmm these are really good," Jelina said.

"Lemme try one," Mondeus reached over.

"Ouch!" he exclaimed as he burned his mouth on a hot nut once again.

"Poor baby," Arielle teased.

Soon they were all munching away on Wiffle nuts and washing them down with fruit juices that they brought from Aqualon. Nobody had any new ghost stories, so they bantered idly for a while.

"This cave is probably several hundred thousand years old," Xander pointed out.

Mondeus, not to be outdone, proudly claimed "I am sure it is more than a million years old. I researched the rock formation on Riad before we left Aqualon."

"That is likely as Riad had much more water earlier in its existence," Xander concurred.

"I didn't realize old rocks were so romantic," Arielle said dryly.

Xander smiled knowingly. He got the message.

The campfire was burning a bit lower now and it did feel cooler in the rocky cave. The stream gurgled and it added a pleasant sound to the ambience making them sleepy. They had had a long day and did not object to Xander's suggestion that they all get some sleep soon. They pulled their well heated sleeping bags closer and found comfortable spots around the fire. It was very peaceful here. It was like what a vacation should be. It made the long trek to the Ixodia system all the more worthwhile.

II.

Mondeus was brooding today. Something was amiss. He did not know what. The others knew that Mondeus brooded more than the average person. They accepted that. They knew he had instincts that were not always explained by routine physiology. Premonition?

Mondeus just knew how he felt and was somewhat oblivious to the precipitating event. Many times he did not know what caused his moods. They just seemed to happen. Often in relationship to a non-descript event. Things that most people would ignore. Yet, it would seem very clear and significant to Mondeus. He often appeared flummoxed that other people could not see it.

He had many objections to this second overnight camping trip on Riad. He was finding fault with any and everything. He claimed that he could not carry enough supplies for two days. That it was too long a hike. That it would take up too much of their stay.

He was not a spoil sport and often welcomed spontaneity. But his constant objections and nitpicking were getting tiring over the last day or so. They knew he did not want to leave the ship for two entire days. He had thought that each expedition on Riad was going to be for one night. Just like the first one. No one really informed him of that specific fact, but he somehow got it into his head. It became embedded there. When he found out that they were going to be gone for two nights, he became fidgety and uneasy. He did not think that Xander noticed it. Or even the girls. But they did.

They had learnt to trust Mondeus's instincts. Even when he suggested the implausible, he was often right. Often times, he appeared to have made a mistake but time usually proved him correct. He seemed to have extra senses or planes of perception that were not usual for humans. Utilizing this and his exceptional mathematical ability he had an uncanny way of predicting future events. He had the ability to be able to take bits of seemingly unrelated information, make patterns out of it and project them into possibilities in the future. Some of these possibilities eventually became high probabilities, given time.

How Mondeus came upon this unusual trait, he himself was unsure. It might have just been those many lonely hours he spent in his early childhood. Just him, alone with his thoughts, which seemed to have heightened his awareness. Consequently, when something was brewing he usually picked up upon it. At other times he would miss the most obvious things. Things sitting on the table right before his very eyes. That was an oddity and contradiction that puzzled most normal people. Especially to those who didn't know him well.

Xander was not oblivious to this characteristic of Mondeus. He was usually very tolerant of it. In fact, he had learnt to utilize it positively. Even though he did not have an exact scientific explanation for it, Xander thought that Mondeus's brain was attuned slightly differently. It seemed to be receptive to stimuli that many of them could not detect. The example that often came to his mind was that of dogs hearing high frequency sounds that humans cannot detect, yet they cannot see the most basic colors. It did not mean that the high frequency sounds did not exist. It was just that the human brain could not detect them. This time, however, he felt Mondeus had gone overboard with his concerns and constant objections.

What could possibly go wrong on a trip on this moon? No one lived here. The Pelican 25 was parked in a safe place. They had adequate supplies. They had mobile devices with them and communication to the inhabited moons. Many visitors have come to this moon before. Mondeus would be wrong this time. He was just annoying and perhaps even showing a tantrum. They were on the verge of telling him to snap out of his gloomy and pessimistic mood.

Both days and nights so far, on Raid, had been pleasant enough. If anything, they were uneventful. After the camping trip on the first night on Riad, they had returned to the ship for couple of hours, picked up supplies and had gone exploring again. They explored a few caves. One had an underground stream and another had an unusual moss growing on its walls. It did not seem to require sunlight to flourish. There was a lot of chatting and idle banter. Nothing out of the ordinary. Mondeus participated but seemed reluctant and often detached.

On the second afternoon of this second overnight trip, they made their way back to the ship. Moving at a very comfortable pace, they would get there before sundown. Mondeus was still uneasy. As they were within a few hundred meters of the ship and had the safest trip possible, Xander concluded that Mondeus was mistaken. This time, anyway. Still, overall, he was right more often than not. They had left the Pelican 25 just around the next hill. It was sandy terrain with not much shrubbery to hide it from their view.

As they turned the corner from behind the hill, they all gasped. Stopped suddenly in their tracks and gaped. They stared and stared.

Rubbed their eyes and stared again. Surely they must have taken a wrong turn. They must have lost their sense of direction.

The ship was *missing*!

Gone.

Completely missing. Vanished into the thin air. As if it was never present.

Xander was the first to react. He tried to radio contact the ship. No response. He did not seem shocked but he was. He wanted to give the appearance of calm. So he tried again. Again, no response.

III.

A few moments passed.

They still could not comprehend what their eyes were seeing.

"We must have taken the wrong way," Jelina finally said.

"I thought this was the right place," Xander answered.

Mondeus had already started to look around and behind them. A few more moments passed.

"I suppose we could have taken the wrong way," Xander said somewhat hesitantly.

"Let's look at the map again," Jelina suggested.

Xander took out the large map of the area and they all crowded around it.

"This is the route we took to go camping," Xander said, tracing it on the map.

"This is the path we took to return," he continued.

"The landing site was just beyond these three large hills," Jelina said tapping on the map whilst pointing to the hills on her right. "I remember them clearly when we got back the last time."

"So do I," Arielle concurred.

"I think we are at the right spot," Mondeus concluded after looking at the map one more time.

Panic was beginning to creep in now that they had confirmed that they were at the correct location. If they were in fact at the landing site, then what had happened to the Pelican 25? It was slowly starting to sink in that the Pelican 25 was indeed gone. And they were stranded!

They looked at each other in apprehension. Not sure of what to do, Xander tried the mobile communication devices again. Still, no luck. He kept trying even though he knew that it was getting futile. Their portable devices could only contact other moons in the Ixodia system by relaying *through* the ship. On its own, it did not have nearly that type of range. Its main use was to maintain contact with the ship and with each other on a particular moon *not* Inter Lunar communication. And its power source whilst quite long was not indefinite.

To say that they were in a spot of bother was a gross understatement. Thoughts flashed into their heads but none of how to actually find the ship.

They walked around for a few hundred meters. In all directions. Like if the Pelican 25 was dragged away by some giant land animal, and they would find it close by. All to no avail.

No one knew what to do next. Xander understood that they were looking towards him for guidance. It went without saying. He was, after all, the leader of this small unit. Mondeus was still fidgety though he said very little. He often became quiet and fussed about non-descript things at times like these. It was his attempt to deal with such situations. His actions were transparent to all but himself. They let him be. Arielle looked as if she wanted to cry. Jelina's expressions were hard to read. Xander showed no outwardly worry but they all knew that inside his brain was racing. Trying to come up with plausible explanations and solutions. So many questions kept going around in their heads. They had not yet fully digested the implications of this dramatic turn of events.

"Safety, as always, first," Xander said with apparent calm. They looked at him trancelike. What was he was talking about? His words seemed distant. It was as if they had all forgotten how to speak and someone suddenly found his voice.

"What do you mean?" blurted Arielle anxiously looking around.

"It will be dark in a couple of hours," Xander continued. "We need to find a place to stay for the night. Preferably a cave. Something that will shelter us. And offer some warmth and protection from the colder winds of the night."

"We do have our warming suits," Jelina said, trying to sound encouraging. She was referring to the gear they took along on the camping trip. It doubled as a heating blanket, using stored power, and was quite handy.

"That's good," Xander added "We would like to use them sparingly though."

At this point they all realized what he was saying. Their supplies and power, including that of the radio devices, were very finite. They would only last a few days. Food was even in shorter supply. They had packed only enough for the two day camping trip. And had consumed the majority of it.

Xander took out the detailed land map of Riad once more and pored over it. This time only Jelina came over to look. Other than Xander, she seemed to have recovered the most from her shock. Somewhat more quickly than the others. Mondeus was still fussing about why they had parked the ship in such deep sand. And why they should have chosen a different landing spot. Arielle finally came over and began looking at the map with Xander and Jelina.

"There are several caves within a five mile radius from here," Xander indicated.

"The closest is about two miles but it says here that it is very small and the roof is not totally of rock."

"Meaning that there is a possibility of collapse over time," Jelina inferred.

"Correct. It also has a single small entrance and no water," he added, as he continued to study the map.

"There is another one over here. Directly across from this low hill to our west. It is about three miles away and seems to be quite large. There are lots of details on this map. There is also water nearby," Xander informed them.

"Looks like a winner," Arielle smiled thinly.

"Interesting choice of words," Xander responded with the tension on his face beginning to loosen up. That was the most relaxed statement by any of them in the last hour or so.

"It will take us about an hour to get over there, at a brisk walk," Xander urged.

"We'd better get going soon then as we would like to be there before dark," Jelina added.

"Yes, yes," Xander agreed. "It will give us some time to scout the area too."

"We will spend the night there and get some rest," Xander said.

"And then what?" Mondeus demanded. The child in him was getting the better of him at this time. It was understandable under the circumstances. He was under a great deal of stress. They all were.

They ignored him as if they did not hear his question. They had no answer to the question but did not want to face the question either. How could anyone have predicted that their ship would go missing? Not a communication system. They had several back ups on the ship. Not a malfunction. Not technical problems. The entire ship with all its auxiliary and emergency equipment. Gone.

"And then what?" Mondeus repeated even louder this time.

Instinctively they all looked to Xander to provide a response.

"And then, we explore all our options," Xander said very slowly and evenly. This had the desired effect. It reassured them just enough to keep them optimistic.

"Come on," he said as they headed towards the cave for shelter for the coming night. Unexpected and unplanned as it was, it was going to be their home for this night. They were all afraid to think, *and how many more nights?*

IV.

They reached their destination without too much difficulty. Because of the low hills they could not see the original landing site that the Pelican 25 had occupied. They were all guilty of looking back at the beginning of their trek. As if the same magic that caused the ship to disappear would make it reappear. Not surprisingly Mondeus did this the most.

"This is smaller than I expected," Jelina said referring to the cave as they quickly looked around.

"That's good. It is safer that way," said Xander.

They all wanted to ask—safer from what? But no one voiced this concern even though they were all thinking about it. The moon was not inhabited and hence the only human life here was that of occasional visitors. There were no large animals either on this moon. Other than natural disaster, what was there to cause danger? That was perfectly logical reasoning before the ship disappeared. Now every improbable event seemed possible as that line of logic had been clearly obliterated by the disappearance of their ship.

"The map lists two entrances to this cave. There may be more. There is also water deeper in the cave," Xander added.

"Two entrances?" Mondeus asked looking around anxiously. Mondeus often behaved much older than he was but on occasions, especially when he was scared he went in the opposite direction. They knew he was anxious and that was not even taking into account that his robot and friend, Tytum, went missing with the ship. Mondeus didn't say it again, but how he wished he had taken Tytum with them on the camping trip.

"I'm tired," Arielle voiced. She looked it. Her hair was unkept and small strands stuck to her face, aided by perspiration. She wanted a hot shower and some rest. Forget the hot right now, she would settle for any kind of shower.

"I think we'd better settle down and get some rest," Jelina said.

Xander nodded. They had found a low shelf in the cave and were going to spend the night here. No time for fire tonight. They would depend on their heated clothing and sleeping equipment.

"Just a quick council before we collapse into sleep," Xander said. He knew that they had an extremely long day and would fall asleep the instant they laid down. But his brain was still working overtime to find options that would help them. They all looked up with some anticipation. As if Xander was suddenly going to give them the answer they badly needed. The answer to the to the question that they couldn't shed from their minds. What happened to the Pelican 25?

"We will take a good night's rest," Xander continued "In the morning, we can have breakfast from the extra food from our trip. Then we will walk back to the landing site."

"Why?" Mondeus blurted out the question they all had in their minds.

"Why?" repeated Xander slowly.

He was not sure if there was a reasonable answer to this question. He did not want to silence Mondeus with a "Why not?"

They were all on edge and he had to show some restraint and composure.

"Because," he started slowly "because we may have missed something this evening."

"Like what?" Arielle asked in earnest. She was also looking for guidance and did not mean in the least to sound short. She could only think that there was no ship and they could not have missed the *whole* ship.

"I am not sure." Xander replied with utmost honesty.

"Maybe we will find some evidence of why the ship was missing," Jelina said trying to help.

"Maybe some other visitors might land there," Mondeus said with a curious burst of energy.

"Perhaps," Xander said. He did not have the heart to tell Mondeus that the chances of this were slim to none. There were relatively few visitors to this moon and it was a rather large moon. Visitors could land on pretty much any part of the moon they wished. To have more than one set within a few hundred miles of each other would be extremely unlikely. Yet it was one of those remote and unlikely scenarios that gave them hope.

They had relied on a communication system that was very dependable. It had an extremely long range and several layers of back up. Problem was the entire system was missing as it was part of the ship. The devices that they carried need the ship to act as a relay station to transmit to long ranges. *Who could have envisioned and planned for such an eventuality?* Xander thought. *Nobody. Just nobody.*

"We must get some rest and set out early in the morning. We should turn off our mobile devices for the night to conserve power. They will not last longer than a week without recharging," Xander said.

They agreed but Jelina spoke up "Shouldn't we keep one of the mobiles on in case someone is trying to reach us? We could take turns at switching on one for each night."

"Good idea," Xander concurred. He noted with some satisfaction that Jelina was already planning ahead. The prudent thing was to conserve all resources.

Another question appeared in all their minds but no one was brave enough to voice it. How many nights would they be marooned on Riad? It was too much for them to digest in such a short time. Even though their brains were preoccupied with their predicament, tiredness eventually got the better of them. Without exception, they fell into a fitful sleep. Among Mondeus's many bizarre dreams, he dreamt that he was trapped in a well. And that the air was in short supply.

V.

Light seeped through the opening of the cave. It was already quite bright outside. Xander, as expected, was the first one to awaken. It was a bit later than he had hoped but they were all exhausted from the night before.

He looked around. The others were all sleeping. Mondeus appeared to be muttering something in his sleep. Jelina and Arielle looked as peaceful as ever. He got up and shook them gently. Then he shook Mondeus.

"Where are we?" Mondeus asked, rubbing his eyes. No sooner than he asked the question, he realized where they were. And what had happened. And that his dream was not much worse than their situation. This still felt like a dream. Perhaps he was having a dream within a dream. And when he awoke it would all go away. Or so he hoped. Xander was under no such illusions.

"We will set out in the next hour or so," he informed them. They all remembered clearly now the conversations from the night before. None of them seemed to be in the speaking mood and nodded glumly. Xander knew he had to keep their spirits up. And with that their hope.

"It will be cooler today than yesterday," he added. Even though the nights on Riad were cool, the days could be hot as there was not that much vegetation. The sand reflected a lot of the heat from the dual suns. It was quite hot the day before, as they had trekked back from camping.

Jelina understood what Xander was trying to do. Turning in the direction of Arielle and Mondeus she said, "I saw some unusual flowers last evening. On our way here." She knew that both Arielle and Mondeus were interested in exotic plant life especially flowering plants.

"You had time to notice that yesterday," Mondeus grumbled. It was more of a statement than a question. It was going to be tough to get

Mondeus in any kind of sociable mood. Their situation was desperate and Mondeus was a thermometer. At the moment he did not conceal much.

"I noticed a few too," Arielle smiled lightly.

"There were a couple of strange plants. With large, indigo colored flowers," Arielle elaborated.

"OK," Xander said "Let's see what we have in terms of food. I think the water in these caves is potable."

They rummaged through their packs. They did not have much food at all. They had some dried fruits and some nuts. A small amount of bread and just three cans of animal protein. A bit of pie and some candy. Some fruit juices. Vitamin pills and a few other basic medicines. That was it! They did not carry too much on the camping trip because of the weight concerns. And because they were not expecting to be away from the Pelican 25 for more than two days!

So dried fruit it was for breakfast. And very little conversation to wash it down with. Soon it would be time to set off again. *Thank goodness there is an abundance of water here*, they thought. Without that their situation would be far more critical. The water in the cave was cold but refreshing. Splashing on the face and washing hands would have to take the place of hot showers. Life was being reduced to its basic elements again.

The trek back to the original landing site of the Pelican 25 seemed a bit shorter than it was the previous evening. Maybe they were too burdened last night to know how far they had walked. They were a bit apprehensive as they came around the last of the low hills. They did not know what to expect. Although, none of them including Xander would admit it, they were all secretly hoping that they would see the ship in the landing area. Like if by some mistake it was invisible the previous evening. Or that they had missed the exact landing spot and would see it just perched in the clearing in this mid morning sun.

No such luck! The landing site was still empty. They walked over it. They did not bump into anything.

"No chance of it being invisible," Arielle uttered with just a hint of seriousness. Just enough as not to make her comment amusing.

They looked around unsure of what they were looking for.

"Why aren't there markings of where the ship was?" Mondeus asked. No sooner had he asked the question he realized the answer. Nonetheless, Jelina answered for him

"Too much wind," she said "markings like footsteps would not last 24 hours in this sand."

"Did anyone notice any footprints yesterday evening?" Arielle asked. She was so preoccupied with the missing ship that she had not consciously looked for any. The lighting was poorer at the time. Footprints would have been less readily visible.

"I did not," Xander said.

"Neither did I," added Jelina

"I see didn't see any either." Mondeus chimed in. They all turned and looked at him. In some way, they always underestimated Mondeus. He was so busy complaining and grumbling that they did not think he had any time to notice anything. Xander should not have been surprised. Mondeus often had his logical brain engaged even when he was doing something puerile.

Again, they walked around for a couple hundred meters to all sides. No sign or clue of the Pelican 25. They rested under some small shrubs when the suns got directly overhead. They had a small bite and drank lots of water. They hoped it did not have toxic contaminants. Nor microorganisms that would cause them to get sick. It was a risk they had to take now, anyway. *It tasted good enough*, Mondeus thought.

"We need to scout around some more before we return to the cave," Xander said.

"And feel free to check out the beautiful flowers," he added, attempting to be positive. Even though Mondeus and Arielle had looked at quite a few earlier, it held their interest just briefly. Nor did it cheer them up.

Xander was beginning to feel desperate now. Patience he told himself. Something will work out. He tried to reassure the others but his voice was not very convincing. He tried all their wireless devices again. Several times over. No response. Nothing.

"There doesn't seem to be anyone within a couple hundred miles of here," Xander said. "At this time anyway," he added. He was hoping for some blind luck. That despite the odds, some other visitors were within communication range. It seems as if that would be an immediate solution to their woes. And in no time help would be on its way. He tried his best to hide his disappointment.

Xander started to think of what his father would do in a situation like this. He knew one thing for sure, his father would remain calm. He wracked his brain for ideas. Nothing new was coming. Finally he said, "We will split up in two groups and walk about 1000 meters in opposite directions."

As if on cue, Mondeus asked "Why?"

Xander was waiting for this. "So far we have all been searching as a group. This will give us the opportunity to explore a larger area."

Jelina wanted to ask him what they were looking for. Other than the obvious, of course. She kept quiet. She guessed the answer would be anything that would give them a clue to the disappearance of the Pelican 25.

"I will go with Arielle; Mondeus, you go with Jelina," he continued. "We will meet back here in an hour."

Mondeus wanted to say he preferred to go with Xander but he knew Xander would not agree to let the girls go alone.

"Okay, we will see you soon," Jelina said.

"Good luck," Arielle said as they set off in separate directions.

Their tedious search began as the suns were descending.

Xander and Arielle were quietly pensive for a while. Finally Arielle broke the silence.

"What do you think really happened to our ship, Xander?" she asked.

She was sure that Xander had already given this subject much thought and would have some plausible ideas.

"I am really not sure Arielle. It just seems as if someone flew away with it or the earth just opened up and swallowed it," he said glumly.

I've rarely seen Xander at a loss for an explanation, Arielle thought.

"It just disappeared without a trace. We have no clues to hint at what likely happened."

Jelina and Mondeus, now some distance away in the other direction were not particularly talkative either.

As expected Mondeus was the first to speak.

"Why did we get the hilly side?" he complained to Jelina.

"I think the other way is just as hilly," Jelina reassured.

"No," Mondeus muttered.

"Let's keep our eyes open and hope we find a clue to help us find the ship," she encouraged.

"I miss Tytum," Mondeus stated out of the blue.

"I'm sure you do," Jelina consoled, having realized that Mondeus was quite worried but wouldn't express it openly.

Time passed slowly but still not a clue. Not a hint of the whereabouts of the ship. Nothing at all. Both teams walked up the side of the surrounding low hills and looked around. Not a thing. One hill did seem to be steeper than the rest. Mondeus and Jelina circumvented this one as it would slow the progress of their search. They had gone a fair distance and were just contemplating turning around when they heard a scream. A sharp, loud scream. In an instant they recognized the voice. It was Arielle's. Then another cry, like someone in pain. Then silence.

Mondeus and Jelina looked at each other in fear. They turned and started to run in Arielle's direction even though they could not see her. About a minute passed. For the moment they forgot that they could reach Xander via the mobile devices. Jelina's mobile device cackled. She grabbed it and answered. It was Xander. As always his voice sounded calm.

"Come over here. I need some help," he stated.

"What happened?" Mondeus asked tersely.

"Arielle fell into a deep hole. It was hidden. Covered by vegetation. None of us saw it," Xander reported.

"Is she alright?" Jelina asked, unable to keep the worry from her voice.

"I pulled her out of the hole but she seems to have fractured her ankle," he said tersely.

"We will be right there," Jelina said hurriedly.

"What will we do now?" Mondeus asked, his voice quavering over the static of the mobile devices.

"She is in a lot of pain. We may need to carry her." Xander answered, still trying to sound calm.

VI.

Arielle was unable to stand much less walk. Her ankle was already swollen and red. It was tender to touch and it appeared to have been fractured. They had been going downhill on a gentle slope. A hole that was overrun by vegetation was part of the geography. Entirely covered and unbeknownst to all. Xander was walking on her left side and completely missed the concealed danger. As she moved forward, Arielle's left foot stepped on air beneath the thin foliage. Her body followed.

Even though the hole was less than three feet deep, the damage was swift. She had fallen forward and landed on her left foot. At a sharp angle on the rocky floor of the hole. Xander had pulled her out quite easily. She now laid on her back crying in pain as Xander looked on helplessly. All he could do was to wait for Mondeus and Jelina to help. When he touched near her ankle, she howled in pain.

It was one of those rare moments when he felt completely powerless. He almost wished it was his leg that was injured. That way, he could bear her pain. He tried thinking of what he could do. He gently elevated her injured foot despite painful protests by Arielle. He remembered that he did have some basic medicines in his kit. They were more like headache type pain killers. Nevertheless, he gave her two with a swig of water. It helped him as much as he hoped that it would help her.

It seemed like a long time but it was less than 10 minutes when he saw Mondeus and Jelina coming over the top of the low hill. Jogging and out of breath, they made good time.

"We got here as soon as we could. What can we do?" Mondeus panted, stating the obvious.

"She seems to be in a lot of pain," Jelina stated looking in the direction of Xander. Without pausing, she turned to Arielle

"How are you feeling dear?"

"It hurts. A lot," Arielle said her face showing much distress.

"Poor baby. You will be OK," Jelina empathized, her face clearly showing her concern.

They were all thinking *"We need a doctor."*

As if reading their minds and responding to their collective thoughts, Xander said, "Now we all get a chance to be doctors and nurses." He was trying to be light, but his comment did not garner much support. Mondeus seemed to be the least enthused about the idea.

"We will have to change plans," Xander continued.

"What do you mean?" Mondeus interjected without giving Xander enough time to elaborate.

"I mean that we'll spend tonight in the closer cave. The smaller one. Instead of the one we were in last night."

This time Mondeus held back his expected "Why?" Xander explained nonetheless. "Because, it would be easier to carry Arielle to that one," he continued.

"I can try to hop on one leg," Arielle offered hesitantly.

She tried to sit up as she spoke. She grimaced in pain with the effort. They reluctantly assisted her up and tried to support some of her weight. She couldn't. Just the jarring from hopping caused too much pain. After a few tries and a very short distance, she agreed to give up the effort.

Next they tried to carry her. It was cumbersome. Xander held her under her arms. Mondeus lifted the uninjured leg and Jelina tried to support the other leg. They walked side by side but it was especially difficult going uphill. Jelina could not get a good hold as she did not want to make contact with the injured area. They took frequent breaks but they knew two miles was a long way. The gentle slopes of the hills appeared much steeper now. Let alone the fact that they still had their packs with them from their now ill fated camping trip. They could not afford to dump their precious little supplies. In addition Xander had chosen to carry Arielle's pack.

"I'm sorry. I'm sorry," Arielle kept muttering.

"It's OK. You'll be all right soon," Jelina tried to soothe her.

"It's not your fault Arielle. Just an accident," Xander consoled.

As they made their tenth stop or so within a half of a mile, Xander realized that they had to come up with some ideas. They would not make it before nightfall to the cave at their present pace. Not to mention that, himself included, they were tiring rapidly. He did not want to have an open meeting about this. Arielle was already feeling guilty. She felt as she was the sole reason of their current predicament.

He asked them all to open their packs. Too tired to ask why, they complied. He went through everything. Took his extra shirt from it. Took a scarf from Jelina's pack. Took out the lightweight folded material they used as sleeping mats from their camping trip. With a knife and some strips of clothing he put together some stringy rope. He then constructed a makeshift stretcher using parts of the mats and the rope he made.

They then placed Arielle on it. With Xander holding two corners of it, Jelina and Mondeus the other two, they resumed their trip. It was easier than before but still quite a task. A task that stretched them to their physical limits when they were going uphill. Despite the frequent stops, it seemed as if their load was getting heavier by the minute. Xander considered discarding some of the contents of their packs. He thought better of it as they still had no idea when they would get help, if at all. They plodded on. They had no other alternative. They could not leave her behind. It was starting to get cooler already and the nights could be downright cold.

* * * * *

"How much farther do we have to go?" It was Arielle in a weak voice this time instead of the usual questioning by Mondeus. The meaning and the context were also entirely different.

"I estimate that, we have, just over half of a mile," Xander panted in short bursts. Just the effort of speaking was almost too much for him. Arielle sensed that. There was no reply from either Jelina or Mondeus.

The reason was obvious. They were too physically fatigued to muster enough breath to speak.

Xander decided that they should take a short break yet again, to catch their collective breaths. The suns were very low in the horizon now. It would be dark in less than an hour. One of Xander's many worries was coming to fruition. They would not get to the cave before dark. Sure they had flashlights but the terrain looked completely different in the night. They had never been there before either. In addition, the makeshift stretcher was literally splitting at the seams. Twice already they had to stop to reattach the scarf that was used as improvised rope.

"I will try to hobble," Arielle said, a bit firmer this time. They all looked at her in surprise.

"You tried that already. It didn't work," Jelina said softly in a not too reprimanding tone.

"I feel a bit better now," Arielle said. "I think the medications have helped a little"

"We will give it a try then," Xander said. He knew that any help that they could get was badly needed, given their present circumstance.

They assisted Arielle to her feet once again. With a heroic effort she tried hobbling on one leg with Xander supporting the opposite shoulder. Gingerly at first, she made a few small steps. Grimacing silently, with the effort and pain, she kept going. With a superhuman effort she continued on. *Take ten steps,* she told herself. *Then ten more,* as she urged herself on. It was still incredibly difficult but just a little less painful than the first time. Maybe the pain medications were having some effect. But most importantly, Arielle also knew that they needed to make it to the cave before dark.

VII.

It had gotten dark by the time they reached the area where the cave was located. According to the map, anyway. Their progress had been excruciatingly slow. They could not have made any better time. It was a testament to the extraordinary effort by Arielle that they even made it at all. They had all seen a toughness of character in Arielle that they had never seen before. She was always so jovial and light hearted that they rarely saw the steely determination that they witnessed in the last few hours. Sometimes the most difficult situations in life seem to unearth the depth of character that most do not even know exists within them.

"It should be around here, according to the map," Xander said.

"I don't see any cave here," Mondeus said bluntly.

"We have to look for the entrance," Jelina added. "It is definitely part of this hill. We will find it soon."

With just a flashlight, the cave was proving more elusive than they had anticipated. Xander had known that this was a possibility and thus his insistence to get here before dark. Yet, he had hoped that they would find it without too many problems. With a single small entrance to this cave according to the map, they would need a bit of luck to find it quickly. He pulled out the map again and began studying it with the flashlight. The others crowded around him to see if they could assist. It was getting colder as the sandy moon's surface quickly cooled after sunset.

After several minutes, they resumed their search for the entrance to the cave. Arielle was left propped up on the makeshift stretcher, as she could do little to help. Xander had given her a second dose of pain medication as she had overexerted herself trying to hobble on the injured ankle. The pain had returned in all its fury. With very little to do, she continued to study the map as the others looked for the entrance of the cave. Many minutes passed. Fifteen minutes, perhaps thirty. It seemed like hours but still no luck in finding the cave. The temperature continued to drop in the open terrain. The wind was slight but even that made it feel colder.

"Over here, I think I see something," they heard Jelina say. They rushed over to investigate. She had found a small opening under some thin vines on the hillside. They quickly pushed it apart but alas, no luck. The passage ended a few feet into the hillside. This was no cave.

For some strange reason, Arielle's mind drifted to her parents. For an instant she saw her mother making pancakes in their kitchen at home. *It's odd how one starts to go back and think of their parent's care, in times of distress,* she thought. She was getting close to despairing. She could not even help them with their search. She knew they were all dog tired. All she could do to help was to continue to study the map. It was quite detailed but it did not give the kind of details to find the entrances of small caves, even though it showed the existence of the caves.

As she kept looking at the map, she conceived an idea that could possible help.

"Mondeus," she called out, with some effort.

"Be there in a minute" Mondeus thought she needed some assistance and hurried over to help her.

"Look here," Arielle said as Mondeus appeared over her shoulder to once again study the map.

"What am I looking at?" he asked.

"I think we can make an estimate of where the cave on this hill is by aligning a few other pointers," Arielle said pointing to the other hills on the map. Mondeus quickly realized what she was saying. Instead of searching the entire side of the hill for the entrance, they could minimize the search area to a small one. This could be deduced by finding a point on the map where they could align the three other visible hilltops and conjure a view that could only be had from the site of the cave. At no other point than the cave would one get these specific views and angles to the other hilltops. They continued to look more closely at the map before calling Xander and Jelina over.

Xander was pleased with these deductions and appeared once again to be optimistic. They had to find the cave soon. It was getting colder despite their warming suits. After some more discussion they all set out to the area just about fifty meters away that they deduced that the entrance of the cave would be located. They had to be correct this time. Surely, their luck had to change. The last thirty or so hours they could not have predicted with a lifetime of planning. Something had to go right sooner rather then later. Their lives literally depended upon it.

VIII.

"Please, let this be it," Xander whispered to himself, as he saw what looked like an opening on the hillside.

They had followed the map to a tee and reached the point where the three hilltops were visible. Surprisingly, this represented a much smaller area than they had anticipated. One had to be at almost exactly where they were to see all three at the same time. If you went as little as forty meters to one side, one of the hilltops became obscured by the side of the very hill that they were exploring.

Xander honed his flashlight to the area where he thought he saw a break in the thin shrubbery as he moved towards it. Mondeus and Jelina followed him. There it was. A small entrance that disappeared into the hill. They finally found it.

"Thank God," Jelina said.

"Finally," Mondeus sighed.

Arielle also exhaled loudly, slumped not too far away from them.

Xander breathed a sigh of temporary relief. He knew that they needed some luck to find this in the dark. At last they had gotten a break.

"I will go first" he said. "Jelina, you can follow me. Mondy, can you kindly stay with Arielle for a few minutes?"

Xander, with Jelina in close tow, made their way cautiously forward. The roof of the cave was low and the entrance was narrow. One could easily be claustrophobic in such a space but they continued on watchfully.

"Not as rocky as we would like," Jelina said, remembering their earlier conversation about the caves.

"No," Xander agreed dolefully, thinking of safety as always.

The tunnel snaked deeper into the hill and suddenly they were in a cavern.

As Xander flashed his light around, it seemed as if they had come to a large room. The ceiling was easily twenty meters high and better than thirty meters length and breadth. More importantly, it seemed rocky on all sides including the ceiling.

"This is it," Xander said. "This is where we will stay for the night."

"Good. I was getting worried about the size of this thing," Jelina finally voiced her thoughts.

Turning around quickly, they headed back to the entrance. Straight to Mondeus and Arielle who were just about getting concerned as they anxiously awaited their return. With some effort, they managed to take Arielle back to the wide area of the cavern. As they scattered the contents of their packs and grabbed a quick drink of water, Mondeus voiced their thoughts.

"I'm tired. I want to sleep," he mumbled.

"Go right ahead," Xander motioned to him and Jelina.

"I want to take another look at Arielle's ankle first."

Jelina, the ever-dutiful sister offered "I will help you."

"Ouch, ouch," moaned Arielle as they removed the bandaged that they had used to wrap and support her ankle. It was angry red and swollen. Some areas were already turning blue from blood that had seeped into the tissues.

Gingerly Xander took his index finger and touched areas of the ankle methodically. Up and down. Side to side. Arielle gritted her teeth and held her breath.

Xander had had some first aid training. He was trying to determine if the ankle was fractured. Certainly there was no bone protruding. That much was obvious. And to be one hundred percent certain, they would need a radiograph of the bone. That could have been done on the Pelican 25.

No need to think of "what ifs" now, Xander thought. The Pelican 25 seemed as far away as a hospital right now.

"What do you think?" Jelina asked softly.

"I think that she may not have a broken bone after all. There is no discreet point tenderness where the bones are. There are also relatively small areas of blue. This suggests that not much deep bleeding took place."

"So that's good news?" Arielle half asked, half stated.

"Somewhat," Xander said.

They had imagined that it would be great news but reading the expression from Xander's face they could see that he was not too thrilled. He knew they were perplexed, so he continued.

"I think you tore the ligaments. Whilst this might not be as bad as a broken bone, that can often need realignment and even surgery, ligament injuries can be severe. They can easily take three to four weeks to heal."

"We would need to immobilize it and you would have little or no use of the leg for at least the next week or two. Using it would make it worse, and exacerbate the pain," he continued, directing his statement at Arielle.

Arielle's face fell again. Xander knew that she already had two doses of medication in the last few hours but he suggested she take another dose. That would give her a chance to sleep and allow the body to recuperate somewhat.

Xander and Jelina found a few of pieces of sticks close by. Water must have flowed through here at sometime in the past. It would have had to, to hew out this large rock. They propped Arielle up and used pieces of string to immobilize the leg. Arielle's eyes were half open by the time they were finished. Apparently the medications also had sedatives properties. They hoped that the pain relief would allow her to get some much needed rest.

They heard some snoring. Mondeus was fast asleep nearby. Xander and Jelina made themselves as comfortable as they could and tried to join him.

Tomorrow will surely come. And hopefully new ideas, it would bring.

Mondeus was very restless. They all had disturbed sleep but Mondeus kept getting a recurrent dream. A couple of times he woke up and thought someone was trying to contact him. He knew reception would have been difficult in this cave but it seemed so real. Arielle slept and woke up frequently. The pain was still there. She was waking up every one to two hours and on one occasion, she even dreamt that she didn't injure herself. Reflexively she reached for her left leg. The splint was still there as was the pain. She had kept a bottle of water close by. During the early hours of the morning, she took yet another dose of pain medication.

As a small amount of light filtered into the cave via the tunneling entrance, Xander and Mondeus got up. Mondeus told Xander about the recurrent dream. As he was recounting it, Mondeus took out his wireless device and looked at it. For what reason, he did not know.

To his amazement, there was a recent entry there. They retrieved the time. It was received at 0200 hours this morning.

No message. No numbers. Nothing at all.

It seemed as if someone had tried to contact them. More specifically, contact Mondeus. And had aborted or changed his or her mind after a few seconds. An empty screen. A blank message!

Xander quickly checked his device. Then Jelina's. Then Arielle's.

Nothing. No entries.

Quite by accident they had left the devices on. With all that was going on last night no one had remembered about turning them off to save power. Fortuitously, as it turned out. But there was no entry on anyone's except for Mondeus's.

Very puzzling indeed, Xander thought.

Was someone trying to reach us?

Xander didn't think that was likely.

Why would they?

No one would know of their plight on this moon. These devices could not be reached from another moon without the ship relay. They were not due back for some days yet. The more they thought about it the more baffling it became.

Even though none of them had said it, they were all thinking that the Pelican 25 was gone. Gone from Riad. Perhaps on another moon or even out of the Ixodia system by now. Why and how, they did not know. But the facts and evidence was indisputable. It was nowhere to be found. Security codes or no security codes, it had disappeared. That much was an irrefutable fact.

IX.

Food was definitely a big concern now. They would be fine with water as it was abundant on this moon. With a few pellets added for purification they could make do. They nibbled at the scant leftovers for breakfast. There were no large trees on this moon. And none of them were familiar with the native vines and shrubbery to know if any of its meager fruits was edible. Trial and error could prove disastrous as some of these could indeed be toxic.

No one said very much. Their situation was beyond sobering, and desperate would not be an inappropriate word. In addition, looking for help on foot was out of the question, as they were now severely restricted by Arielle's injury. Even Xander had to make an extreme effort to break the silence. Like any good leader he asked,

"Any suggestions on how to proceed today?"

They were all quiet.

"Come on. Anything at all. There must be something we overlooked," he urged.

"We could go back to the Pelican 25 landing site," Jelina said.

"What for?" Mondeus interjected.

"I am not sure," Jelina answered honestly with a slight shrug of her shoulders.

"*Could* we have mistaken the landing site and got lost?" Arielle asked softly, her pain still very much evident.

"I thought of that a few times," Xander said. "I really don't think so."

"We used the map. Everything checked out. We all recognized the site. And we even used that as a point of reference to find this cave."

"I guess you're right. I was just hoping," Arielle said quietly.

"If we go back to the landing site, someone will have to stay with Arielle," Xander said looking alternatively from Mondeus to Jelina.

"I would be OK by myself," Arielle said, not too convincingly.

"We don't need more than two people to go back there," Xander replied, somewhat more firmly now.

Jelina would have volunteered but she knew her brother often counted on her calmness in difficult situations. So she did not want to rule herself out of this mini-expedition.

"I will come with you," Mondeus said. He did not want to stay all day in the cave and he did have that little thing about Tytum in the back of his mind. His buddy, Tytum, was still missing. Some activity was better than inaction, as far as Mondeus was concerned. He could not remain in one place for an entire day. Especially given their circumstances. He was already very fidgety. Further containment would only increase his anxiety.

"OK then, it is settled," Xander said. "Mondy and I will leave for the landing area in a short while."

They made rapid progress to the original Pelican 25 landing site. It was still early in the morning and cool. With nothing to hold them back, it seemed to be a relatively short distance. They could communicate with the girls by the wireless devices. But with power resources now coming into the picture, they had decided to keep their sets on, whilst the girls kept theirs off. In the case of an emergency, Arielle and Jelina would call them. The best they could do was to leave a message for the girls. Measures had to be taken. Who knew how much longer they would be on this deserted moon?

Mondeus finally spoke as he strode alongside Xander.

"It's not looking good, is it?" It was more of a statement than a question. Xander could still be surprised at the fluctuations between Mondeus's behavior. At times, like now, he appeared wise beyond his years, having full grasp of their dire situation. At other times, he would fuss about a trivial matter that seem entirely unrelated to their present situation.

"Where there is a will there is a way," Xander replied trying to sound confident. "We have to take one day at a time. Maybe someone will try to find us."

"Do you think your father will try to find us?" asked Mondeus with a trace of hope in his voice.

"Very unlikely at this point," said Xander. "He wouldn't know yet that anything had gone wrong. The ship is only required to file a log every forty eight hours *during travel.* We are expected to be on this moon for at least a week. As far as everyone is concerned, we would ask for help if needed. Only problem is, we have no method of asking for help."

"If we don't return to Aqualon after about a week or more, it is possible that someone trying to contact us from the System may get concerned. And perhaps try to locate us by raising an alarm with the authorities," Xander said, trying to sound optimistic.

"And no one in the Ixodia system would try to find us?" Mondeus stated more than asked.

"Not really. They have no reason to look for us," Xander continued. Then realistically, he added "Problem is we have no food, hardly any supplies, very little power and Arielle is badly in need of medical attention. I think we have to leave this moon in the next day or two, otherwise…." He trailed off and did not finish the sentence. He did not need to. Mondeus was in his adult mode.

"I tried a few times to contact Tytum," Mondeus said on a seemingly unrelated topic "but no luck."

Xander knew that Mondeus was trying to tell him that another possible glimmer of hope had subsided. He was not surprised. The Pelican 25 could easily be hundreds of thousands of miles from Riad and Tytum might as well be in another galaxy.

They reached the area where they had left the Pelican 25 almost four days ago. There had been no miracle. No ship to be seen. They hardly expected that anyway. Xander suggested that they started at the distant end of the clearing and walk the full length of it to the base of the low hills, then retrace their steps alongside their original path and repeat this process. After several such trips they could literally cover every square meter of the clearing. They were not sure of what exactly they were looking for. Any clue would be of help. It was slow and tedious. More importantly, it was uneventful.

A couple of hours had passed and they were about to quit the process when Xander furrowed his brow.

"Come over here," he said to Mondeus, in a tone that made Mondeus look up quickly. He was only a few meters away and they were in the far corner of the clearing where the two sides of the low hills met.

"Do you notice anything?" Xander asked.

"Not really." Mondeus was looking around intently.

"Look at the sand," Xander said "Nothing unusual?"

"I don't see anything," Mondeus said almost despairingly.

"The sand seems to have been disturbed."

"Disturbed?" Mondeus asked rhetorically.

"Well, sort of. It looks different from last evening. This particular area," Xander explained.

"I am sure we walked passed here late yesterday afternoon, when we were carrying Arielle. The sand here was wavy like the rest of the clearing. This corner of the clearing is somewhat protected from the wind. By the hillside. So it takes time for it to get wavy if it were recently disturbed."

"Go on," Mondeus urged.

"Well it seem as if it has been flattened! Probably disturbed and then leveled again as not to look unusual," Xander said incredulously.

"What for?" Mondeus asked now very puzzled and somewhat scared.

"Even more confusing is that it had to have been done last night!" Xander exclaimed.

"Because when we passed here last night it was wavy like the rest of the clearing."

"But there is no one here," Mondeus said, looking around rather frightened.

"Well someone or *something* was here three or four days ago. That much we know. Why not last night?" Xander asked. He was speaking as much to himself as he was to Mondeus.

A thousand questions came to his mind. Nothing seemed to make sense anymore. It was the same for Mondeus. Everything was bewildering. And they had neither answers nor explanations for any of it.

X.

Mondeus and Xander sat in a corner of the clearing for several minutes without saying anything. They had discussed this new finding with Jelina and Arielle via the mobile devices. They agreed that someone must have been here a few days ago. But last night? That made no sense. Xander, who rarely second guessed himself, was starting to wonder if he was mistaken. Mondeus did say he noticed the change in the sand pattern as well. So surely, it could not be just his imagination. Or did he influence Mondeus into believing that?

The questions were unrelenting. *How? Why? What?*

As they continued to ponder their current state of events, Xander finally spoke. "We'll camp here tonight."

This time he got the expected "Why?" from Mondeus.

"If someone was here last night, it's possible that they might return tonight. If that's the case then we might be able to get some help. The least they could do is allow us to use their relay, to get help from Aqualon."

"I see," Mondeus nodded.

"We do have to return to the cave to get some warmer clothes and something to eat," Xander added.

"I could go alone and return in about an hour," Xander suggested.

Before Mondeus could interrupt, he continued, "I would like one of us to be here all the times in case someone shows up."

Mondeus looked around nervously. Xander noted his behavior but was still hoping he would agree. Mondeus finally said. "What do I do if it is *something?*"

Xander realized that he would not be able to convince Mondeus to remain alone. He also knew that it would be difficult for Mondeus to carry everything from the cave that they needed to camp overnight in the open. He had a decision to make.

It was taking a chance that they could miss the window of opportunity. They would monitor the clearing for the next few hours and then return to the cave together. With a quick turnaround, they would only be away from the landing site for about two hours. Not a bad plan really as he wanted to take another look at Arielle's ankle. It would also allow the suns to be lower in the skies as it was quite hot now.

They communicated the plan to the girls via the mobile devices. Xander wanted to spend as little time in the cave as possible before they returned to the landing site. They sought some shelter in the thin shrubbery. The suns were almost overhead and it was very hot now. They had water but it would not have been enough to last for two days if they had decided to stay here overnight. It was just as well that they needed to return to the cave. They could now use as much water as they wanted.

Mondeus and Xander continued to try and make sense of the recent intrusion of the clearing. The only thing that they could possibly connect is that whomever was here last night also used an electronic communicating device. This would explain the entry on Mondeus's unit. Still, there was no one in sight or any firm evidence that anyone was nearby. Just as puzzling was they had tried to raise anyone within range. A couple of hundred miles at least, without any luck at all.

Xander could be patient when he wanted. He concentrated on his task of monitoring the clearing. That was a bit tougher for Mondeus. He easily lost his focus when there was no immediate goal. However, all things considered, he was showing remarkable restraint given their desperate situation.

Xander was also a bit concerned about leaving Jelina and Arielle alone in the cave overnight. Especially since Arielle was injured and effectively immobile. But in the end it had been a clear choice albeit a tough decision. As undesirable as it was, he had no real alternative. All of their lives depended on being able to get some help soon.

XI.

Mondeus spoke little. He was busy trying to keep pace with Xander as they moved quickly in an effort to return to the landing site as soon as possible. The few extra pounds he was carrying did make a difference in this heat. He made a mental note to watch his diet and exercise more frequently when he returned to Earth. It still startled him to think, *if* he returned to Earth.

Matter-of-factly, Xander stated, "The power in our sleeping units is running low. We need those to keep warm in the night. Especially for Arielle, now that she is ill."

Mondeus knew Xander was worried. He could not remember ever seeing him this worried before. Even though Xander's voice seemed well under control, Mondeus detected an undertone of concern and urgency in every sentence. This spilled over to him as he could sense Xander's feelings. No doubt their situation was very grave.

"I'll take a look at them when we get there," Mondeus stated quietly. "I have an idea."

Xander did not ask what idea. He had to trust his group now. He would need all the help he could get from them. He would not be able to get them out of here by himself. And at the back of his mind, he knew that Mondeus was a technical geek. He would figure out something.

They reached the cave without too much difficulty. Given their recent excursions, an uneventful journey was welcome. Welcome they were too by Arielle and Jelina. It was as if they had been gone for a week. Arielle had a smile on her face but effort it took showed through. Jelina had already prepared what could be crudely called a meal for them; from the scraps of food they had remaining.

Xander headed directly to Arielle's side. It pained him to look at her in so much distress. He again almost wished that he was hurt instead. So he could bear her pain for her.

"How are you feeling?" he asked softly.

"I just took some more pain medication. About an hour ago," she stated thinly, forcing a smile.

"That is not what I asked," he prodded gently.

"I have had better days," she responded quietly. He could see the pain in her eyes.

"Is it the pain?" he continued, sounding more like a caring, probing doctor.

He had touched her forehead and found it to be quite warm. He was almost sure that she had a fever. It was difficult to tell as the cave was warm in the day. He did make mental note that Arielle appeared be cold yet she was warm to his touch.

"She has a fever," Jelina said quietly. "She has gotten more flushed since this morning. And she wanted to go back into the sleeping units, even though the cave was quite warm."

A sure sign of a fever it was. It was unlikely that this was some virus that she picked up in the last 24-48 hours. More likely and much more worrying was the ankle injury was somehow related to her temperature.

Xander was gently unwrapping the bandage now. Arielle protested faintly and then added, "Since this morning my ankle has been throbbing. The pain seems to be more throbbing in nature."

That bit of information was very relevant to Xander. He all but knew what he was going to see as he unwrapped the last of the bandages. The entire foot and the lower part of Arielle's leg was red in color. Quite a dramatic change from the last time Xander saw it. He touched the red areas. It was hot. He touched the areas higher up the leg. It was not quite as hot. It was quite obvious that Arielle's leg was infected. Somehow, she likely sustained a break in the skin when the ankle was injured. Bacteria had entered. Most likely Strep and now the entire foot and the distal part of the leg was infected. Arielle needed medical care as soon as possible. More specifically she needed antibiotics. They had some basic antibiotics on the Pelican 25. For all practical purposes, that was like saying that they had some antibiotics on another planet.

Their situation seemed to be getting worse with each passing hour. Xander knew that without medical attention, there was a real chance of death in the next few days. Arielle's medical condition had worsened dramatically. *What misfortune! As if being stranded on the deserted moon was not bad enough. Now this!* Xander thought.

Mondeus seemed oddly detached from this particular situation. He was sitting close by, yet he did not even join in the conversation. They knew him well enough to know that it was not for lack of concern. In fact, if anything, it was because he was too concerned and could offer not any help. It was his way of dealing with it. Almost a form of denial.

As they sat there, silence briefly took the forefront whilst they wracked their brains. For some outlet, some solution, anything at all that would help. Mondeus suddenly interrupted, "I got it."

"Got what?" Jelina and Xander chorused. Arielle was too weak to join in.

"I think I can recharge the sleeping units," he said.

They waited for him to continue. He did.

"I looked at the power pack in the unit," he said. They noted he had opened one of the sleeping units with a small multipurpose camping knife. "With a little bit of time and some luck, I think I could get them to recharge using solar power."

"Great!" Xander said, not doubting for a moment that Mondeus was technically skilled enough to pull it off.

"How long would it take?" Xander asked.

"About an hour for each unit, given the quality of tools I have."

"Well, thank goodness," Jelina said. *It was about time that something went their way,* she thought.

"Ok then," Xander continued. "We'll leave in about five minutes. We will take our units and Mondeus can work on them when we get there. When we return tomorrow, he can work on the other two."

Xander was pretty sure that given the fact they had two suns, they would be some warmth in the early part of the night in the cave. It would cool off in time but much slower than in the open. That was the pattern last night. Much more pressing was Arielle's deteriorating condition. It was going to be even harder than he had thought to leave Jelina and Arielle overnight. He still had no real choice. Difficult decisions had to be made. He plowed ahead with their plans. Hugs were exchanged. Few words were said as Mondeus and Xander left for the clearing again.

XII.

Xander and Mondeus reached the original landing site of the Pelican 25 with minimal delay. The suns were still high in the sky, allowing Mondeus to begin working on the power device in their sleeping units. He spoke little while he worked. Xander was deep in thought and chose not to disturb him.

They were seated in the low shrubbery at the far side of the clearing. That was where the bushes were tallest to provide some shelter from the suns. They could also look directly at the other side of the clearing where the sand had been disturbed. They did not speak about it nor discuss it. It seemed as if their choice of sitting some distance from that area was driven by some subconscious fear. This was not unexpected given the series of astonishing and completely unpredictable events that had transpired over the last few days.

Xander's thoughts returned to Arielle. He was extremely worried about her. He knew that humans had a remarkable capacity to survive. His reading of Earth's history told him that it was just about a millennium ago that humans first discovered antibiotics. Many millions had died from infectious diseases in their history that they were powerless to cure. In fact, just a few years before antibiotics were discovered, tens of millions of human had perished worldwide in a great influenza pandemic. Given the population of Earth at that time, it was a disaster of unimaginable proportions. Second only to the use of weapons of mass destruction.

He had also read about the agonizing wait for the fevers to break in infections like pneumonia. This was also prior to the advent of antibiotics. It was at that point, after an insufferable wait, that humans knew whether their loved ones would survive. He was not sure if the same pattern would be true of the infection that Arielle had. Maybe the micro flora on Riad were different to those a millennium ago on earth.

There must be something he could do. He thought of using microbicides from plants. He looked around. There were a large number of cacti looking plants. He was sure some of them contained antibiotic like substances. He was also sure that some of them contained chemicals that were toxic to humans. Which was which? He had no way of knowing. In desperation, he tried the mobile devices again. In vain. No answer. Worse yet, it seemed as if there was no hope of an answer.

Back in the cave, Jelina was also worried. She also knew their situation was dire. She knew she had to stay strong. It was her role to take care of Arielle. That would allow Xander and Mondeus the best opportunity to seek help for all of them. She was afraid now. She was also afraid of tonight. Not so much of being alone in the cave with Arielle tonight but what if something was to happen to her. Sure she could contact Xander and Mondeus by the communication devices but what could they do if Arielle took a turn for the worse. She was a bit heartened when Xander made the decision quickly to leave them in the cave. Initially she took that to mean that Arielle's condition was not grave. When she reflected on it later, she was not too sure. Xander often made difficult decisions quickly if the alternative was not a reasonable one. She did not need to look far for an example. It was very recently when he did not bother to even rouse them as he averted potential disaster in colliding with an asteroid.

"Jelina, I am still thirsty," she heard Arielle whisper. She was awakened from her thoughts and quickly moved to give Arielle more water. She had done this less than half an hour ago. She made a mental note to leave a lot of water beside Arielle overnight.

Arielle's lips were dry and cracked. More from the sustained fever than anything else. The pain medication may have also contributed to it. Her voice was weak. She had no appetite. Jelina had insisted that Arielle have some juice. At least that had some sugar content. Arielle needed her body as well as her mind to fight this illness. For as long as possible. She held out hope that they would be rescued. And she surmised that their chance would increase with each passing day.

Arielle felt a lot of pain in her leg. She also felt pain in her mind. Being immobile and in pain was not the worst of it. Somehow, she felt as if she had doomed their chance of being rescued. Finally, with a great deal of effort, she spoke. "Jelina, I am not doing well."

"I know dear," Jelina concurred.

"I think you should go," Arielle continued.

"Go where?" asked Jelina

"You can leave me here. Go with Xander and Mondeus," Arielle whispered insistently.

It slowly dawned on Jelina. Gradually at first, but she soon realized what Arielle was trying to say. Arielle did not want them all to perish because of her condition!

Jelina eyes went wide. She saw the pain in Arielle's eyes. She also saw that Arielle was completely honest and selfless.

"Not a chance!" Jelina said firmly.

"You could move quickly. And look for help," she paused for breath "if, if I were not, with you." She finished the sentence just short of exhaustion. It took that much effort out of her.

"We will NOT leave you here," Jelina said resolutely, with some degree of finality in her voice. She could not bear to even consider the words "to die."

"Let alone, Xander would never agree to any of this," Jelina continued steadfastly.

At the mention of Xander's name, Arielle felt an even greater pain. It was more jarring and it was in the region of the heart. She did not want to die. She also wanted to be with them. Her guilt had gotten the better of her temporarily.

Jelina took a piece of fabric, soaked it water and gently mopped Arielle's forehead. She was sitting alongside Arielle. It pained her to see her best friend like that. They had been closer than sisters in the last couple years.

"You are very brave," Jelina soothed.

Arielle did not seem to understand the context of her statement, so Jelina elaborated, "You were very brave to ask that we leave you behind."

Arielle nodded. She was afraid of speaking as she was very close to tears.

"You can go at anytime," she finally sobbed.

"I will manage," she continued, none too convincingly.

"I want you to understand that there is very little we would gain from doing that," Jelina said slowly.

"How?" Arielle managed.

"If we walked for a few days, the most we would cover is a hundred miles. That hardly increases our chance of finding anyone to help. Our communication devices would have picked up anyone within a few hundred miles already, anyway. Let alone, we could go around in circles, have no place to stay overnight and run out of water," Jelina explained. She realized that she was starting to sound like her older brother. *After all, we have a lot of genes in common,* she thought.

"I see," Arielle finally conceded. Some of the weight lifted from her chest. With that the pain in her leg became more apparent.

"Arielle," Jelina said tenderly.

"Yes?"

"You are a brave and determined girl."

Arielle nodded.

"I want you to use all your determination and all your mental energies. To get better. Please, we know you can do it."

"I will," Arielle said at long last.

The sunlight had all but receded from the entrance of the cave. It would be night very soon. It was not the time to think about hostile aliens, monsters or creatures of fantasy, Jelina reminded herself. It was time to remain calm and logical. It was time to use all the stored knowledge of thousands of years of human evolution to survive. It was time to just endure the night and see the light of the next day. A day that she hoped would change their fortune.

XIII.

They decided that they would both stay awake for the first few hours of the night and then they would take turns sleeping. Mondeus was not particularly talkative but rather surprisingly, seemed not in a pessimistic mood. It was almost as if he expected something good to happen. Xander could not see any imminent reason that would allow their situation to improve dramatically. He concluded that Mondeus was probably pleased that he had fixed the power in their sleeping units or he was now warm and comfortable. More than likely, both.

Yet, Mondeus had often not only been a thermometer of their feelings, but a beacon that frequently pointed the direction in which they should look. Mondeus himself, more of a science student than one of literature had once eloquently summarized this quality in an old Oscar Wilde's quotation "A dreamer is one who can find his way by moonlight and his punishment is that he sees the dawn before the rest of us." Xander was very surprised when Mondeus had said this and had never forgotten it since. He was not only surprised by its content, as it was shown time and again to be true. He was more surprised by the amazing insight that Mondeus possessed.

"I am getting sleepy," Mondeus mumbled to Xander.

"I think it is OK for you to go to sleep now," Xander replied. "I'll take the first watch and wake you in about two to three hours."

"Thanks," Mondeus muttered, almost sleeping already.

In a few minutes, Xander heard the monotonous light snoring of Mondeus. He looked so peaceful sleeping, with just his head visible from the sleeping bag. It was as if he did not have a care in the world. Xander had a warm protective feeling towards him as he would have had with a younger brother.

He decided to try Jelina on the mobile devices. She was also sleeping and was alert in a flash. If he did not know his sister well, he would have bet she was awake when he called.

"Anything?" Jelina asked anxiously.

"No. Nothing yet," Xander replied.

"I just wanted to check on Arielle," he said softly, not wanting to disturb Mondeus.

"She is very ill and had some shaking chills about an hour ago. After that she dozed off," Jelina said, hardly able to conceal the worry in her voice.

"I see," Xander said slowly. He had very little else to offer.

"Mondeus?" Jelina asked.

"He is sleeping," Xander said "I am taking first watch and his turn will be in a couple of hours."

"I wish I was there to help you," Jelina said, even though she knew that she could not leave Arielle. She knew she was needed just as much here.

"I'll check in with you before dawn," Xander continued, "Please call if things change."

"I will. Love you," Jelina said signing off. She knew that when Xander said things changing, he meant if Arielle deteriorated further.

Too many thoughts flooded Xander's head now that he was awake alone. Firstly, his brain tried to come up with solutions and scenarios for their rescue. He kept going around in circles with this and kept getting stuck. Even though he tried his best to find new ideas and solutions to their present problem, his mind kept going back to the actual disappearance of the Pelican 25. And he would get into a quagmire at that point. He finally shook his head. Visibly, as if to get his brain untangled. And then he decided to give it a break.

Gradually his thoughts shifted to his home and then to his father. He thought of his father sitting in his study on their modest home base orbiting Earth. It first brought a warm feeling to his heart and a smile to his face. Then a pang of distress as he realized that his father was most likely still unaware of their current plight. His pain became even greater when he thought that he and Jelina may never see their father again. No, he must not think that way. He must stay positive. Where there is a will there is a way. He tried to convince himself that they would get off this moon. Even if it took weeks.

They would be missed eventually and a search party would be sent, he reasoned. He had no doubt that his father would come to this moon in an effort to find them if it came to that. But that may still be a week or two away. His father was not a big risk taker. He trusted them with responsibility and Xander felt it was his duty to live up to those. Even though he had little control of the circumstances they now found themselves in. He must keep them alive. Help would come. Hopefully, sooner rather than later. His heart fell again when he thought that help would come eventually but would it be too late for Arielle?

Again he could not shed these dark thoughts. His mind drifted to how his father would feel if they did not make it back to the System. Would he be able to cope? The loss of his mother had already taken a toll on him. Even with his clinical mind, Xander did not think his father would be able to withstand the loss of both of his children. That would be too much for any human to bear. It was like the proverbial bad nightmare that he could not wake himself from. Only difference is, it was him who was awake and Mondeus who was sleeping. *I must not think that way,* Xander kept telling himself. They would be rescued. Soon. And all would be well.

He looked over at Mondeus. Mondeus looked as content as a baby with a pacifier in his mouth. It was usually the other way around with Mondeus worried looking and fretting and Xander calm and collected. It was almost time to rouse Mondeus. That he duly did with some difficulty. Mondeus had a weakness for sleep. He did not function optimally without being fully recharged. After some grumbling, Mondeus finally sat up and leaned against a small smooth rock as he prepared to take watch. Xander reported that the night had been uneventful so far. Tired, he tried to sleep after doing some slow, deep breathing to clear his mind.

Mondeus looked around the dark clearing. There was hardly any wind at the moment. Nothing moved. Very little sound. It was quite cold but he was well protected in his unit. After several episodes of looking around with absolutely no sound nor movement, his eyelids began to feel heavy again. He tried his best to keep them open. It was his turn to keep watch whilst Xander got some much needed sleep. His eyes were burning. He nodded once. Reopened his eyes and was not sure when he finally dozed off.

Mondeus eyes reopened as sunlight streamed over the horizon. He realized that he had dozed off. For how long he was not sure. There was still no sound nor changes to his surroundings as far as he could see. He felt guilty as he realized it was past the time he was supposed to hand over to Xander.

Xander was stirring as well. Even before Mondeus could call out to him. He looked at his watch and noted the time. He looked over to Mondeus. Before he could make a comment, Mondeus decided to come clean.

"I fell asleep," Mondeus stated, a bit ashamedly.

Xander did not answer but looked around some more.

"I didn't mean to," Mondeus continued.

This time Xander did answer.

"I know," he said quietly.

He did not seem too perturbed. He looked around the clearing one more time. It was almost fully light now. He saw no changes that would make him think that anyone or anything was here overnight. The sand did not seem to have been disturbed at all. Xander also thought that if there was any unusual noise he would have heard it, despite his light sleep.

It was about that time Mondeus checked his communication device.

"Look!" he said sharply.

Xander immediately came over as Mondeus tone was both excitable and urgent.

There was another entry on his device. This time the entry was clear. Tytum had tried to contact him. The questions all came at the same time.

"It is clear that Tytum is still on Riad," Xander voiced. "And likely within a few hundred miles too!"

If that is so, is the Pelican 25 still on this moon too? Xander thought.

So many questions and so few answers. Xander started to reconsider the unlikely possibility that they were somehow lost and had returned to the wrong clearing. None of it made any sense. He looked around. He had to believe his eyes. They were at the original landing site of the Pelican 25.

They all recognized it. They had used this as a reference point for finding the cave that Arielle and Jelina were in this very moment. Yet there was no Tytum nor Pelican 25 here. But Tytum was somewhere in their radio range. That much was certain. *Should that make us optimistic?* Xander thought. At least, it was something to hold on to for the moment. Mondeus thought so too. After all, his pal was apparently not lost forever.

XIV.

"I knew he was still here!" Mondeus could not contain his excitement.

Xander did not ask why as they walked rapidly in the direction of the cave.

Mondeus was, of course, referring to Tytum and the events of the night before.

"I am not sure why he didn't contact us before," Mondeus puffed as he tried to keep pace with Xander, who was going pretty quickly now.

"I am also puzzled by that, though it appears as if he did try," Xander said finally.

"You mean, the other night in the cave?" Mondeus eagerly continued.

"Yes," replied Xander.

"That would mean he was here all along," an excited Mondeus said almost to himself.

"Or he was here, left and returned last night," offered Xander.

"Oh," said Mondeus, as he had not previously considered that possibility.

"The bigger question is," Xander paused for a moment.

"What?" Mondeus could not wait.

"The bigger question is," Xander continued as if he had not been interrupted, "whether Tytum is still with the ship."

Again, Mondeus seemed a bit surprised. He thought aloud "Why would he not be with the ship?"

"It's likely that he is, but we have to consider the possibility that whomever took the Pelican 25 could have discarded him before leaving the moon."

"Why would they do that?" Mondeus persisted.

He could really have tunneled vision at times, Xander thought. He tried his best to be patient as he did not want to dampen Mondeus's newly found optimism.

"I am not saying he is not with the ship. All I am saying is that we need to still conserve our resources until we find the Pelican 25," Xander explained.

"I see," Mondeus said slowly. *Xander could be such a pragmatic person at times,* Mondeus thought. It took the excitement out of situations. But Xander was correct. Hearing from Tytum was not the same as getting rescued and Xander could not afford to be wrong. Too much was at stake.

For once, Mondeus decided to reflect on this. Maybe it was the gravity of the situation that caused him to do it. Maybe he was just too tired to converse. Even Jelina and Arielle had jokingly accused Xander, at times, of being too logical and taking the fun out of things.

It must be very hard on Xander, Mondeus thought. Xander wanted the same things they wanted. He, more than anyone else, knew how gravely ill Arielle was. He wanted them to be rescued as desperately as anyone else. But he could not afford to abandon reason and caution at the very time they needed it most. Under extreme stress, most would. But not Xander. He was not programmed that way. He had to stand guard. For their collective well being. And temper his own excitement throughout. He wondered why he had not seen this before. He also wondered if Jelina had seen this point of view or even the fun loving Arielle. He was not sure he wanted to be Xander right now. It must be tough to be him. Although secretly, he hoped one day to be like Xander.

They were approaching the cave again. Since they had done this a few times already, they had no problems in finding their way. Xander had communicated the good news to the girls that they were contacted by Tytum. Jelina was very excited and had all the questions they had asked themselves. But mixed with the good news was grave news.

Jelina relayed to them that Arielle had taken a turn for the worse. She was barely conscious now. She had high fevers and chills. She was breathing very shallowly. It was because of this that Xander had decided to return to the cave and offer whatever assistance he could. It was because of this that he knew that if they did not get help within the next 24-48 hours, Arielle would most likely die. It was because of this he knew there was absolutely no margin for error. Xander had more than enough reason to be overwhelmed as he was beset with their dire plight.

XV.

"Xander, Xandy," Arielle whispered faintly. It was almost inaudible and Xander was not even sure if she was aware of their presence.

Her breathing was shallow and frequent. Not the long deep breaths one often associated with comatose people. But short, shallow breaths. Most likely due to the high fevers. Her lips were dry and cracked. Some strands of her hair stuck to the side of her damp face. She did not move save for her chest moving up and down with each breath.

Xander and Mondeus were too shocked to say anything at first. Arielle had deteriorated significantly since they last saw her. That was less than 12 hours ago. Jelina had used some of the stretcher fabric to elevate the upper part of Arielle's body. Propped her up a few degrees, so that she was lying on a gentle slope. It seemed to aid her breathing efforts. From time to time Jelina mopped her face with a wet rag. It was soothing as well as it kept her cool. She was very hot now. Jelina told them that she had had rigors and chills overnight. Xander was surprised that Jelina did not ask them to abort their watch overnight. And return to the cave in light of Arielle's grave condition. Only slightly though, as he knew that his sister also saw the big picture. They had to get help soon otherwise Arielle would perish. There was not much more that Xander and Mondeus could do at the cave. In so many ways his sister was just like him, he thought.

Mondeus knelt at the left side of Arielle legs. Jelina was also on the left side as she occasionally mopped Arielle's face. On Arielle's right, Xander sat and reached over Arielle's forehead. He stroked her forehead gently, using only two fingers of his right hand. He sensed more than saw that Arielle had awakened. He continued stroking her forehead and he felt a slight touch on his right thigh. She had voluntarily touched him! His spirits were lifted.

"Arielle, can you hear me?" he whispered firmly. No response.

"Arielle, can you hear me?" he whispered even firmer. He felt the light touch from her right hand again. She was acknowledging them!

And as if in slow motion, she opened her eyes gradually. As if to remove any doubt, they all saw her nod her head ever so slowly. She was indeed hearing them and for this they were happy. Yet it was extremely painful to watch her in this condition.

They were all but out of the useful medicines. Their First Aid kit was rather basic. A few of the pain killers remained but Arielle didn't appear to need them now in her altered state of consciousness. Xander decided that he will take another look at Arielle's leg. He removed the bandages gently. He was struck by how far up the leg the redness had reached. It had crossed over the knee joint and encroached on the lower thigh area. He placed the back of his hand on the red area. It was *hot!* He did not have to be a doctor to know that she had severe cellulitis. And the infection was spreading to her bloodstream causing sepsis. He did not even bother with the ankle now. No one died from a fracture. He just hoped that the bone would not become infected. For the first time, another distressing thought crossed him. Suppose they were able to save Arielle but she lost her leg. He could not even bear the thought of Arielle with one leg. He quickly pushed it out of his mind and tried to return to the present.

"I think we can leave the bandages off," he said to Jelina.

"They don't serve any purpose at the moment," Xander continued.

Jelina nodded. The skin did not appear to be broken and if anything, they were trapping bacteria in the bandages as opposed preventing them from getting into the leg.

"How about a support for the ankle joint?" Jelina quietly asked.

"Good idea," agreed Xander.

Mondeus was quiet throughout this entire period and seemed to be at a loss for words. Arielle appeared to have slipped back into sleep again.

With Jelina propping up Arielle's injured foot, Xander concocted a sling for her ankle. He tried to make it loose as not to impinge on the blood flow of the leg which was already very swollen. Yet firm enough to provide some support. Arielle winced a couple of times as they were manipulating the leg. It meant that it was still painful in that area.

"I would like you to check on this every couple of hours or so," Xander told his sister. Jelina had read just enough about gangrene to know the importance of what her brother was saying. She nodded silently whilst wondering if a career in medicine may not be more suitable for

Xander than she had thought, in light of what she had just seen.

When they finished they tried to give Arielle sips of water. They got a few sips past her throat and had to be satisfied with that. She really needed intra venous fluids and antibiotics but that was as far away as Aqualon and the Pelican 25.

* * * * *

"When do you think Dad will know that we are missing?" Jelina finally voiced the thought that they all had.

"Maybe in another few days," Xander said quietly.

"Why so long?" Mondeus asked.

They were sitting in a corner of the cave nibbling on the last scraps they had left as food. They did not want to disturb Arielle and were having a council of sorts.

"Do you know how long we have actually been missing?" Xander asked rhetorically.

No one answered.

"In reality, it has only been a few days," Xander said. It had already seemed like an eternity.

"No one would really take notice until we missed the *second* check in. That would be at the 96 hours mark. Central Station would be the first to pick up on this as the automated Pelican logs would be incomplete. Their computers would generate some kind of alert. It would then have to be relayed back to Aqualon. The Aqualon authorities would then have to issue a missing person report before any formal action is taken," Xander explained.

"Why does Aqualon have to be involved?" Mondeus asked.

"Aqualon is the local jurisdiction and I am sure has their own criteria for filing missing people alerts. Unless they were already aware that we had an accident or something like that, I am guessing that it would take another 24 to 48 hours before they launched an investigation on their own. Only then would information be sent back to the system and our emergency contacts notified that something was amiss. Not to mention Father was going on travel just after we left," Xander continued.

"I see," Jelina sighed.

And with that sigh, the unmistakable message was that help from Earth would not come anytime soon. If and when it came, it could be too late for Arielle.

Mondeus digested this too. His next statement may have seemed totally uncaring except to those who knew him well.

"I need some real food to eat," he said absentmindedly.

His comment had nothing to do with their present predicament. Both Xander and Jelina knew it was his way of dealing with their present situation. Mondeus could seem distant at time but one thing they knew for sure, he cared deeply about all of them.

With a heavy heart, Xander outlined their plans for the rest of the day. They would remain at the cave with Jelina and Arielle until late afternoon and return to the clearing overnight to continue to look for help.

Mondeus had tried numerous times to reach Tytum but to no avail. Xander wanted to tell him to save the energy on his communication device but did not have the heart to. He did not want to take any hope away from any of them. Instead, he asked Mondeus to use Arielle's transmitter to try and locate Tytum.

Xander knew it was going to be difficult to leave later this afternoon. Mondeus too. It would also be difficult for Jelina. That was the unspoken thought they all had. And many questions too. Would Arielle still be with them when they returned to the cave? Can Jelina cope with this on her own?

Should they all stay in the cave with her?

He thought of leaving Mondeus with Jelina. He asked her about this.

They decided that Mondeus should go with Xander as Tytum would most likely contact him. Their best hope so far. They had to stay positive. Jelina assured them that she would be all right but she didn't sound or look too confident. She knew they needed some sort of intervention *soon* to stave of impending tragedy. She still felt that way when they departed later that afternoon leaving her as the sole caretaker of Arielle. For some time, she sat down reflecting on their strange predicament. With Arielle sleeping, she was essentially alone. She could not accurately assess her feelings. Perhaps it was because she had never been overwhelmed by so many concurrent emotions. She was anxious and confused at the same time. She felt fear, yet she was still determined and strong. Someone needed her. She felt despair creeping in and managed to push it away. And all through this she felt tender and caring towards Arielle.

XVI.

The clichés were many.

They were in a deep hole. Their backs were against the wall.

Yet none of those seemed to convey the gravity of their situation, as they had been over used time and again in benign circumstances. Theirs was anything but benign, Xander thought.

Mondeus for his part was hoping that this was a nightmare that he would soon wake up from. No such luck. Every time, he fell asleep and awoke they were still stranded on this desolate moon. Why did they decide to come to this moon? Why did this have to happen to them? What could possibly explain the disappearance of an entire ship? Those were the thoughts that kept going around in his mind.

The Ixodia system was considered very safe from all accounts. That is why it was one of the premier vacations areas for younger teens outside of their home system. That was why it had been approved by their parents.

"Tonight is going to be it," Mondeus said almost to himself.

"Hmm?" Xander inquired, looking for clarification.

"I think Tytum will contact us tonight," Mondeus said rather optimistically.

"I hope so," Xander agreed in a more even tone.

And as an afterthought, half-speaking to himself, "Why not today?" Mondeus had no answer for him.

Xander was also hopeful that they would be able to reach Tytum. The more important question in his mind was, of course, "Was Tytum still with the Pelican 25?" They were walking steadily and approaching the original landing site. Xander decided he would not voice this concern with Mondeus. He needed him to remain optimistic. Even Xander had his doubts. Was he really a worry box or was he just being pragmatic? At this time, his emotions were too heightened for him to answer such a question accurately.

Back in the cave, Arielle still appeared to be sleeping peacefully. It was far from peaceful as she was closer to delirium than reality. No doubt her high fevers were causing this. She thought that she saw Xander and Mondeus. She heard Xander and Mondeus. Of that she was sure. Then she dreamt that she saw Xander and Mondeus. Then she dreamt that they left her alone in the cave. And then she had a dream that she was dreaming about them. And then she dreamt that they were stranded in some distant moon and their spaceship lost forever. She dreamt that she was having a dream within a dream. And now she was dreaming that Jelina was calling out to her, calling to her not to go by the river.

Softly at first, and them firmer.

"Don't go," she heard at first.

"Don't go, you will drown," she heard, but she was still heading to the river. Why did Jelina want to stop her? She continued.

All she wanted to do was to get a drink of water. She was thirsty. Her weary legs barely carried her. But she must get to the river. Get to the river to get some water. She kept going. There was a lot of water there. She could hear it. She could see it. If only her best friend would see that, she would surely let her go.

And then the voice changed. It was no longer saying "Don't go."

It was saying,

"Stay with us."

"Stay with us, please,"

"Stay with us, *please!*"

And her eyes opened. And she remembered. Slowly at first, but then more. And more. She was still in the cave. She had injured her leg. She was very ill.

And Jelina was sitting next to her. With her legs crossed in a meditative posture. And was saying slowly to *her*, "Stay with us."

"Water," she whispered.

Jelina's eyes opened quickly and in that instant, Arielle saw worry. She also saw love.

And caring.

And devotion.

For her.

She would not forget that look in a hundred lifetimes. In such a short moment of time, yet she was so sure.

Jelina brought water to her lips. She sipped some. Then some more. Then she drank most of it. Jelina was surprised. She refilled the cup and

Arielle drank some more. She was really thirsty. And more awake at the moment than she had been for some time. Jelina looked a bit relieved. Even the beginnings of a smile to the corners of her lips. Hopeful. Yes. That was more like it.

"Where are Xander and Mondy?" Arielle asked slowly with each word taking a lot of effort out of her.

Jelina seemed to be happy that she was talking but Arielle registered that she looked away ever so slightly before she answered.

"They went to get help." She did not say that they went again *hoping* to find help. But Jelina could not keep her gaze and this betrayed some of the optimism her voice had conjured.

"Oh," Arielle said.

It was difficult for her to say more than single words. Her breathing was still rapid but her consciousness seemed to be much clearer for the moment. Perhaps it was a lull in the fever, Jelina thought.

Jelina continued to talk to her and Arielle nodded her head in agreement and even managed to indicate no at times. Her eyes were open most of the time but they were beginning to close more often now. Jelina badly wanted to share this temporary improvement with Xander and Mondeus but she waited. There would be a lot of time later.

For now, she wanted to stay with Arielle and be that sister for her. The sister she never had. She realized that Arielle was not just her friend. She wanted Arielle to be positive in mind and survive. Hold on to life and live. For her, for Xander, for all of them. For her parents and for what she meant to them. Jelina felt feelings deep within her that she was incapable of explaining with words. It was sort of like her feelings for her brother Xander and her father. She knew the feelings were there but could not correctly describe them. No, it was closer to the feelings she felt for her long lost mother.

As Arielle's eyes closed, Jelina resumed her meditative posture and her even and soothing voice kept repeating positive messages to Arielle. "You will get well soon." "Stay with us." "You are strong." "Hold my hand." "Your mind is powerful." "You are a beautiful person." "We need you."

For some reason, the last one registered in Arielle's mind. And it replayed itself. They needed her and she would not let them down. They *needed* her. She would not die. She would get better. Regardless of the situation. Regardless of medicines. She was needed. By Jelina. By Xander. By Mondeus, by her parents. She not only believed that she would get better now. She knew. And it made her peaceful as she slipped into a deep sleep and started to dream again.

PART 4
Eureka

I.

Xander was sleeping lightly as Mondeus took first watch. Again they had the suspicion that the clearing was disturbed when they had returned. Yet there was no real evidence to support this.

Xander thought he heard some sort of a crackle. He opened his eyes and asked Mondeus if he heard it too. Mondeus shook his head. He closed his eyes again. A few minutes later he heard some sort of static. This time he could pinpoint it. Immediately he asked Mondeus to check his communicating device. There it was. An entry from Tytum. Just a few minutes old. Tytum was trying to contact them again. Maybe it was a remote program that kept redialing. Maybe, he was just out of range and his signal was weak. That would mean it was at least a couple of hundred miles away.

They were both pondering that possibility, when they heard a grating sound. Very clear and coming from their right side. Less than 50 meters away. Unmistakable. Sounding as if some large door from a warehouse was being opened. They did not even have time to fully register the significance of this when they heard another sound. A sound that told them that they were not alone. The sound of excited chattering. The sound of human voices. But a language that they had not heard before.

Mondeus was already getting ready to stand and hail them when Xander motioned him to keep still. He eased back down to the ground, in the short shrubs where they were camping for the night.

"Why?" Mondeus whispered tersely to Xander.

"They may not be friendly," Xander said slowly.

Mondeus took a moment to comprehend what Xander was saying but kept still. And it was during this time that their situation became really bizarre. In front of their very eyes, they saw light coming from the side of the low hill on their right. It was coming from inside the hill. More specifically it was coming from a cave, the entrance of which was now visible.

That was when the grating sound made sense to them. It was a door of sorts. It covered the very large mouth of a huge cave. With vegetation growing on it, one would not even notice it from a few feet away. You would need to literally stand on it to know that there was an opening behind this massive door. With it sloping at about 60 degrees there was not much chance of this either.

The light was very bright and the scene unfolded as one from a movie. One unbelievable event after another. The chattering continued. Clearly a language from outside their home system. And then they saw it.

The Pelican 25.

It was being towed to the mouth of the cave. Xander's heart skipped a few beats. Mondeus's almost stopped. The Pelican 25 glided towards the mouth of the huge cave as if on roller skates. It paused.

And then several humans of short stature emerged from it. From *their* spaceship. The one they had left here just a few days earlier to go camping. Their ship had been stolen. And it was clear that whoever stole it was not from Aqualon.

Xander and Mondeus gasped. They stared in disbelief with mouth and eyes wide open. Mondeus was now glad that Xander's first instinct was caution and he did not rush in at the sound of human voices. They counted six male humans who were milling around the ship talking excitedly. They were all just over five feet tall. Almost a foot shorter than the average human from the System. In fact, these aliens were shorter than all of them. No doubt they were fully grown as evidenced by their body habitus, beards and tone of voice. How many more were there in that huge cave? They had no way of knowing. All they knew was that the Pelican 25 was only capable of carrying eight people on long trips and 10 on shorter trips.

Xander's mind was in a blur yet a lot of things now made sense. Still, he had so many questions. *Who were these people? Where were they from? Why did they steal our ship? How long have they been on this moon? If approached, would they be hostile? And if so, would we be killed or kidnapped?* Xander had no way of knowing.

He had some answers to a lot of his earlier questions now. For starters, they did not get lost. The Pelican 25 was still in the same area they left it. Only some minor differences. It was in a huge cave instead of the clearing they left it in. It was under the command of someone else. Tytum was still with the ship and his intermittent communication was probably due to the fact that he was deep underground. And whoever these people were, they took great pains to keep themselves hidden. They seemed to have some use or purpose for the Pelican 25. And that purpose was being revealed as they watched in astonishment.

As they were literally looking at the ship, which was now parked just a few feet outside the opening of the cave, they noticed flashing lights.

And then the low hum of an engine. Surely, they were not trying to take off this very minute, Xander thought. No, it could not be that. Or could it?

What is there to stop them from flying off with the ship? Xander thought. He was sure that this was their intention. And it could be anytime. Not this minute because the ship was too close to the side of the hill for take off and some of the men were still on the ground. But both of those factors could be remedied in a very short period of time.

As the hum of at least one of the engines of the Pelican 25 continued a few of its external lights flashed, Xander notice a long thin structure protruding from the top of the Pelican 25. It was rising and had a flashing light on its tip so he could track it. It seemed like an antenna of some sorts and rose almost 200 feet in the air. Heading above the low hills surrounding the clearing. Both himself and Mondeus could make a good guess at what was happening. *The aliens were trying to communicate with someone or someplace.*

It must be a long distance away otherwise they should have been able to use the Pelican 25 internal systems. These aliens seemed advanced enough to fly the Pelican 25. And the scary thought was that they could do it very soon.

II.

Xander knew he had to do something. And very soon too. He was scared. So was Mondeus. They had now curbed their initial instinct to hail the aliens. He was almost sure that there presence would put a kink into whatever plans these unusual people had for the Pelican 25.

He was trying to think clearly. With the volume of new information that his brain registered in the last few minutes, that was very difficult.

He whispered to Mondeus to fall back from their current position. For once Mondeus did not ask why but just followed. They dropped back deeper into the shrubbery and away from the Aliens and the Pelican 25.

Xander wanted to talk to Jelina but he didn't want to take the chance of giving up their position. He should not have worried as the wind had picked up. It was going away from the cave that held the Pelican 25. Yet it was prudent to be extra cautious. He quickly relayed to Jelina the salient features of what they had just seen.

Jelina was speechless as she listened. She finally found her voice and asked, "What should we do?"

"I have been thinking about the same thing," Xander said.

"I have an idea," he continued.

"What?" he heard coming from both Jelina and Mondeus, who was crouched beside him.

"I'll try to use the relay in the ship and try to get help from Aqualon," he explained.

"We need to go now," Xander continued rapidly. "I do not want them to take off before we have a chance to try."

"Good luck," Jelina whispered.

And then she added, "Arielle is hanging in there."

With that, Xander was reminded of how critical their situation was.

Mondeus and Xander crawled to the top of a low hill at a comfortable distance from the Pelican 25. Xander noticed that the protruding antenna was no longer there. The ship had not changed position so takeoff was not imminent. But he knew time was of essence. He adjusted his communicating device for long range transmitting. And to use the ship as a relay.

He could feel the tension being emitted by Mondeus. Holding his breath, he tried.

No response.

He tried again.

Still no response.

His heart fell. Mondeus was getting fidgety.

He adjusted the frequency and tried yet again.

But still no response.

He had an idea of what was going on. But his brain refused to accept it.

Yet, deep down he knew he was correct. Mondeus knew too.

Somehow, the Aliens must have reconfigured the communication system of the Pelican 25. And it was no longer able to receive their signals. It seemed to be the only logical explanation.

As they stared at the scene in front of them, they heard the voices again. Sounding as if someone was giving orders. In a moment they knew what it was. The Aliens were moving the Pelican 25 back into the enormous cave. And their leader or someone in charge was issuing commands.

Xander made one final try. In vain.

Mondeus found his fingers. And tried to reach Tytum. A distant crackle.

He was able to get some sound. Very muffled, as his communication device activated. Strange. If Tytum was on board the ship, he was less than fifty meters away. Mondeus should be able to reach "him" easily.

The answer came to him quickly. Tytum was not in the Pelican 25. But somewhere deep into the cave. And as soon as they closed the entrance again, he would most likely lose signal.

They watched the Pelican 25 being towed back into the cave with robot like precision. In stunned silence. Before they could even discuss what they should do next, the grating sound began. And soon the huge doorway was closed again. The ship disappeared. The slope of the hill appeared as if it was never disturbed. It seemed as if the whole episode had *never happened.* It could have been just a figment of their imaginations. There was no evidence to attest to it.

And Xander, Mondeus, Jelina and Arielle were no better off than they were just an hour earlier.

III.

Xander had some tough decisions to make. Should he stay here and try to approach the aliens hoping that they would help?

That seemed highly unlikely given the fact that their ship was *stolen, hidden* and was going to be used for some unknown mission. A secret one to be sure.

Should he return to the cave? For starters, it was still night and finding their way back would be challenging. That was not the biggest problem though. They could leave here and by the time they returned, the Aliens could have left with the Pelican 25.

Another thought crossed Xander's mind. Would these Aliens return to this moon after their trip? Possible, but unlikely. He shared this with Mondeus who responded with his customary "Why" this time. Xander explained the unlikely but possible scenario, that these men could perhaps be smugglers of some sort. That would explain their need for secrecy and could also explain the presence of this *huge* cave, which seemed to be some kind of storage area. Still this scenario left too many questions unanswered. The cave was definitely man made or enlarged by man. For such a large cave it was not listed on the map. And it had a *door!*

Eventually he decided to hold council with Jelina by radio and the three of them decided. Normally it would have been the four of them. In the end they decided to return to their own cave. Jelina argued that the Aliens were probably not going to take off until at least the following night. This was based on the fact that they seemed to have been finished for the night and they had shown no inclination to operate during the day, perhaps for fear of being seen. Her deductions were sound and logical as usual, despite being very strained with Arielle's critical condition.

Xander agreed, but he interjected the possibility that the Aliens could leave pre dawn on this very night even though it would have made sense for the Aliens not to return to their cave if they were indeed planning to depart tonight. Mondeus also thought that the most likely scenario was the Aliens resuming whatever they were doing the following night. With that they made the journey back to their present home.

"Oh Xander, I am so glad you are here," Jelina said with a lot of worry and a touch of relief in her voice. She looked in the direction of Arielle. Arielle was in apparently deep sleep but he knew better. She seemed to be slipping into a comatose state as her breathing had become deeper and slower in nature.

Mondeus muttered to himself, "I'm hungry." This seemingly insensitive comment was not meant to be heard. But Xander and Jelina did hear it and looked at each other. They were hungry too. Sometimes they forgot that Mondeus was younger than them and he was really an overgrown child. When he did act his age they were often surprised given the fact that he was so advanced in many other aspects of his life.

If it were at all possible, their situation was getting worse with each passing hour. There was almost no food left. Just a few scraps that they nibbled at. The power on their communication devices was getting low. They were turning them off alternately to conserve energy. At this time they had Arielle's switched off completely to use as an emergency back up, if it became necessary. Mondeus had taken a look at them and concluded he could not find an alternative source of power for these sensitive and tricky things. He had almost broken Arielle's device in the process. Pretty much they had water and warm sleeping units at their disposal. That was it! Even with the water Xander knew there was the possibility of getting sick from it. Small animals could contaminate it even before it flowed through their cave.

Jelina reacted to Mondeus in a non verbal manner. She moved over and gave him a long hard hug. She whispered firmly to him. "Everything will be all right." He nodded with his eyes moist and cloudy. And he seemed better. And suddenly less tense.

"At least we know where the Pelican 25 is now," Jelina encouraged.

"That is a good start," Xander agreed, also trying to be positive.

Jelina also wanted to hug Xander. But for some inexplicable reason, she found this harder to do. He seemed to understand. With Arielle being so ill, he needed this now more than ever. Yet she could not do it. Their eyes locked. Xander moved over and after a bit of hesitation gave his younger sister a big firm hug. No words spoken. They were too close. They could feel each others feelings and they knew what the situation was. No words were needed.

It was at this moment that Xander made up his mind. He knew what he had to do. It was their only chance. Their only chance to save Arielle. He would do it. Even though he knew he would risk his life and theirs too.

"This might be our only opportunity," Xander said, sounding very determined.

"But that's so risky," Jelina protested.

She initially tried to talk him out of it. But she had no real alternative plan. Mondeus also reluctantly agreed. But insisted that he come along.

IV.

As dusk approached Xander and Mondeus walked slowly back to the original landing site of the Pelican 25. As they neared it they moved cautiously and stayed in the low shrubbery. Conversation was sparse as they did not want to risk being detected nor did they feel like talking.

They need not have bothered as they approached the large Alien cave, the entrance was unopened. They could not even detect the entrance in the fading light even though they were much closer to it than last night. Xander hoped and prayed that the spaceship and Aliens were still there. They had concluded that asking the aliens for help, remote a chance as it was, was the only way to try and save Arielle. A chance that Xander had to take.

Mondeus and Xander settled down in the shrubbery and waited. Waited for the Aliens to emerge from the cave. Nothing happened. An hour passed. Two hours passed and still nothing. They continued to wait and Xander was getting really worried now. Mondeus was starting to fidget.

And then they heard the deep grating sound as they had heard the night before. And the accompanying chatter. The voices seem even more urgent than the night before. Just like the night before the Pelican 25 was towed out but they brought it *much further out into the clearing.*

The chattering continued non stop and the tallest of the Aliens, who appeared to be their leader of sorts, having most of the say. He was giving commands and instructions. Mondeus and Xander could hear the voices but did not understand one word of it. They did see a lot of hand movements that they could relate to. The Aliens moved in and out of the ship. Again they counted six men. Mondeus also noticed that the men were dressed differently from the night before.

"It looks like they are wearing some kind of uniform," Mondeus whispered.

Xander nodded in agreement.

"I am pretty certain that they plan to leave tonight," Xander said.

"The uniforms plus the fact that ship is in a position to take off."

As if giving them confirmation of their intent, the main engines of the Pelican 25 came to life. A deep, low pitch sound that they knew very well. The doors were still open but it was time to act.

"Good luck," Mondeus whispered. He had his communication device in the palm of his hand. He was trying to reach Tytum after their relay attempts through the Pelican 25 had failed yet again.

Xander stood up slowly and Mondeus squeezed his arm for the reassurance of both of them. When Mondeus let go, Xander took a deep breath in and began to walk towards the ship in the clearing.

Out of the shadows Xander moved and in clear view as he came into the area lit by the Pelican 25. He waved his arms in the air, whilst calling out "Hello", "Hello."

At first no one seemed to notice him. The reason registered on Mondeus as he saw the scene unfolding in front of him. The engines of the Pelican 25 were initially drowning out his calls. And suddenly one of the Aliens noticed him. He must have called out to his comrades because they all appeared alongside him in a couple of seconds. Mondeus saw Xander getting closer to the Aliens, still waving his arms. He was still calling out to them. For some odd reason he noted that Xander was a couple of inches taller than the tallest Alien who seemed to be their leader.

It was just about this time, the lead Alien reached into his uniform and pulled something out. He aimed it straight at Xander. In disbelief, Mondeus saw a blinding flash as Xander instantly fell to the ground. In the sand. Slumped in a heap. Lifeless.

Mondeus must have let out some sound. For a split second the Aliens turned their heads in his direction. Mondeus did not wait but began running. He ran and ran. Heading back for their cave. In the dark, he did not know which direction he was heading to. But he continued on. And in his panic to leave the landing site, he had dropped the communication device. Arielle's device. The only one that had adequate power.

V.

Mondeus continued running. He ran until he was exhausted and then collapsed on the ground. As he sat up looking at the sky, he realized that he was totally lost. He did not recognize anything around him. He felt a dreadful sense of horror gripping him once more. His breathing became sharper again. He was in a panic. He urged himself to be calm with little success.

His brain had not fully digested the events of the last hour. Was Xander fatally wounded? Dead? He did not know. He had started running immediately. In what he thought was the direction of the cave. His adrenaline surge gave him energy. He had ran non stop for close to an hour. He was expecting to be back at the cave by now. To tell Jelina and Arielle what had happened. He must have lost his way. In the darkness and in his confused state. The only thing he knew for sure was he was not anywhere close to the cave. He did not recognize anything at all around him.

That rising dread again. He must be having a bad nightmare. He tried pinching himself. It hurt alright. He was awake with a heart rate of about 160. Thumping in his chest. He could almost hear it. "Calm down," he said aloud to himself. *Slow deep breaths,* he told himself. And managed a few. He must think. He must clear his head and try to think. It was the only way. But it was very difficult to do. It seemed as if twenty thoughts were forming in head at the same time. And he could follow none to completion.

Finally, as if by some insight, he realized what he could do. He could call Jelina on the communication device and try to determine where he was. Perhaps she could guide him back to the cave. Why didn't he think of this before? He had no idea. Mondeus fumbled around in his pocket for the device. He could not find it. He felt around again. No luck. In all his pockets. The device was *not* there. He peered at the ground around him. Nothing. The panic returned with such rapidity that he was overwhelmed again. To make matters even worse, he realized that it was Arielle's device that he had lost. The one with the most power remaining. Despair was now stepping in. In addition to his panic.

He tried to retrace his steps for a couple of minutes. He quickly realized this was futile. It was dark. And he wasn't even sure of the direction he came from anymore. His fear intensified. Not only was he lost. He had no way of reaching anyone or anyone reaching *him*. He was completely and totally lost. Riad was a big moon. He did not know what to think. He slumped to the ground once again. And in sheer exhaustion, he fell asleep.

* * * * *

Meanwhile, back at their temporary home, Jelina kept watch over Arielle. She appeared to be sleeping most of the time but Jelina knew better. She was hoping to hear from Xander. After a couple of hours, she became worried. She reassured herself that he would call soon. Perhaps they were still in waiting and Xander wanted to remain quiet. She could not sleep though. With each passing hour, she got more worried. She knew her brother. He would have called by now. He was very responsible and knew fully well the precarious condition of Arielle.

Something must have gone wrong. Mondeus would have called by now. Something must be terribly wrong with them both. And she couldn't do anything about it. She tried to reach Xander and Mondeus. In vain. Again and again. She was reaching the point of despair. She couldn't go looking for them. She couldn't leave Arielle in this condition. So she waited.

* * * * *

Mondeus opened his eyes. Rubbed them open. At first, he did not realize where he was. And then the events of the previous night returned to him. It was not a dream. As much as he wished it to be, it remained with him. And that feeling of hopelessness had come back too.

Daylight was streaming over the low hills now. It was what had woken him up. After a few minutes, he became aware that he was a bit calmer. He could complete a thought. He remembered Xander and he forced his mind to return to the present. He thought of Jelina and Arielle and it dawned on him that they would be extremely worried by now. She would have expected to hear from them. And she would have tried to contact them. Her worry and fear by now would have no boundaries. She would naturally fear the worst since she was aware of the plan to ask the Aliens for help. Although he did not know it then, his thoughts mirrored almost exactly the events that Jelina had experienced.

Oddly enough, this realization of Jelina's predicament gave him courage and strength. He must find her. He must get back to the cave. And let them know that he was alive. And what happened to Xander. They all depended on him now. He must not let them down.

With great effort Mondeus got to his feet. Although, he did not consciously think about it, the thought formed in his mind—what would Xander do in a situation like this? A lot of Xander had rubbed off on him over the years. And he knew the answer. Focus on the present. Focus on now. There must be a way. Where there is a will there is a way, he reminded himself. It was one of Xander's mottos. He looked around at the horizon and hills carefully.

After a few minutes he started to get an idea of where he was. It was fully light now and he recognized the outline of the hills they had used to find the caves. Only problem they were much further away from him than when they were looking for the opening of their temporary abode. He had run a long way last night. And after studying the hills on the horizon for some time, he calculated he had gone off at about 90 degrees to the left of the route he should have taken. He spent a few more minutes gauging his position. And mapped out a route back to the cave using the tops of the hills as signposts. And then, without food, without water, he set out slowly towards the cave looking to reunite with Jelina and Arielle.

* * * * *

The suns were almost entirely overhead when Mondeus reached the cave. He moved slower now from sheer tiredness. As soon as he approached the vicinity of the cave he recognized the immediate area. It had taken him hours walking over rough terrain and he wanted to go as much as possible "as the crow flies." He did not want to take the chance of getting lost again. This meant going over a few hills as opposed to walking around them. That way he could always keep the landmarks in his sight. It seemed like days to him. Last night seemed a long way away. He was not hungry. But he was very thirsty now. It was quite hot.

140

As he reached the entrance of the cave, Jelina rushed out to greet him. She did not ask any questions. She just grabbed him and hugged him tightly. She knew that things had gone terribly wrong. His face said it all. He had small cuts and scrapes all over his body from his battle with the terrain. The result of shrubs, cacti and vines that he had tripped over. More than a few times. He finally whispered through cracked lips, "Water."

She sat him down just at the entrance of the cave in the half shade and went for water. He drank. And then drank some more. His breathing eased a bit and his chest stopped heaving. Jelina looked directly into his eyes and she saw tears clouding his vision. She held him again, like the little brother he was. Still she did not ask him anything. A few minutes passed. Finally, she asked, "Xander?"

The tears flowed freely now.

VI.

The unmistakable drone of the engines of the Pelican 25 seem to be intruding in his dreams. Except it was of a higher pitch. Xander dreamt he was moving very fast. He dreamt that at such speeds his ship would shatter at the seams and kill them all. He knew in his dream that it was not designed to travel so fast. The only time he had heard the engines scream at this pitch was in simulations of emergencies. What was the emergency? Why didn't they slow the ship down? This was madness. Indeed, it was suicidal.

He became aware that he was in a small space. Like a closet. Xander opened his eyes. It was dark. He was really hearing the higher pitched engine sound. He reached out and touched the walls. Both of his hands moved together although he moved only his right arm. Strange.

And then it all flashed into his brain. He was indeed in the Pelican 25. In fact, he was in a compartment of the room that he and Mondeus used as sleeping quarters. Specifically, in the upper level of the Pelican 25. The last thing he remembered was a sharp stinging pain as he was shot walking towards the Pelican 25.

As he became more alert, he felt a general soreness on his shoulders. His arms were stiff. He felt metal on both wrists. He could move his hands and forearms. Only problem, he could move them no more than 12 inches apart. It seems as if he had some sort of magnetic restraints on them. They allowed a very limited range of movement. It was clear that he was a prisoner. Aboard his own ship! It was also clear that this ship was traveling much faster than it was designed to. Perhaps his kidnappers were not aware of that fact. Still, if the ship crashed, they would all be dead.

Xander had a sinking feeling in his chest. He was essentially handcuffed. Locked in a closet. Traveling at a far too dangerous speed. To some unknown destination. In his own ship!

And in the meantime, Arielle was gravely ill. Trapped in a cave with Jelina. On an uninhabited moon. And what about Mondeus? His thoughts again returned to the night before. Walking towards to Pelican 25 for help and being shot. What did Mondeus do then? Was he also captured? Did he return to the cave? Would he be able to find his way there by himself? Was it really the night before that all this happened? He realized that he had no way of knowing how much time had elapsed.

He tried to collect his thoughts. Focus on the positive, he told himself. A little voice kept nagging him from the inside. Asking. What positives could there possibly be in this situation? He had to force himself to quiet that voice. It was not helping him.

Firstly, he was alive. He told himself aloud. And if he was, he could conceivably do something. He was worried about Mondeus and Jelina and Arielle. He should be there helping them. Not trapped here and probably flying to a different system. He would have to have faith. And hope. He had no alternative now. He had to trust that Mondeus would get back to the cave safely. Trust that Jelina would take care of Arielle. And have faith that they would somehow be rescued. He had to try something. Anything but being trapped, unable to move in this compartment. But first, he must stay alive. And for that, he had to act now.

He must warn his captors that they were all unsafe at this speed. They probably exceeded maximum recommended speed for this ship because they had a long way to go. They had likely boosted the engine power and were using measures reserved for emergency maneuvers only. And for *very short* durations. There was no way that they could last very long traveling at this speed.

He tried to call out to them.

"Anybody there?"

No answer.

"Anyone?"

Still, no answer.

"Help."

Silence.

"HELP!"

Just the sound of the engines on overdrive.

Xander listened to the sound of the Pelican 25 engines as one waiting for a time bomb to go off. From time to time he tried calling for help. No one heeded his calls. No one came. Perhaps they could not hear him. Maybe they were sleeping, he thought.

He waited. And waited. He realized he felt somewhat groggy. And had a headache. As well as body aches. He felt as if he was getting some sort of viral illness. But he had no fever. He figured he was probably having some after effects of the stun gun or whatever energy weapon they shot him with.

PART 5
The Gadorans

I.

Xander must have closed his eyes during this interminable wait. Finally, he heard some voices coming up the small stairwell. And then the door of his little compartment opened. Two men were there. He recognized one of them. Their stocky leader, from the night before. He tried to get up with some difficulty. The space was too small for all of them to fit in this small cubicle. They grabbed him roughly by the shoulders and pulled him out of the closet. He almost fell headlong into his own room. The men were chattering rapidly as he had heard them in the clearing before. He had no clue of the language they spoke. It was not even vaguely familiar. Xander was pretty certain that it was not from any nearby system.

And then he saw the reason for their visit. They thrust a small tray in his hands. It had some food in it. Or what looked like food anyway. He looked at it and then looked back at them. They seemed surprised that he did not grab it and start to eat immediately. Xander was hungry for sure but he had something more important on his mind. He needed to tell them to slow the ship down. He tried in the most common Earth language. They looked at him blankly. He tried again in another language. The main one spoken in the Ixodia system. Their blank looks remained. Xander noticed that impatience was beginning to creep into their faces. And they were getting ready to leave. He had to change tactics fast.

With a kind look in his eyes and a polite tone, he pointed to himself and said "Xander." Again they seem surprised. The leader looked at the food and muttered something gruffly under his breath.

Xander pointed to himself again and said "Xander." And tried extending his hands for a handshake type gesture. The shorter man accompanying the leader seemed to understand that this was a friendly greeting of some sort. He responded by touching his forearm against Xander's forearm. Xander smiled.

He was making progress but at this rate it would take a very long time to communicate the limitations of the Pelican 25 to them. For sure, they could not read the instructions from the ship's computer. He tapped his chest lightly again and said "Xander," whilst smiling and looking at the Alien leader. This time he responded and pointed to himself and said gruffly "Bodak." Xander realized that was his name and gently asked "Bodak?" The leader nodded, with a strange combination of impatience and curiosity.

He had heard the name Bodak mentioned by the other man during their conversation but there was a sound before it. Xander figured that may have meant leader or some rank or form of respect. He stuck with Bodak and pointed his ears trying to indicate that the engine noise was too loud. They did not understand. Xander tried using signs and hand gestures in many ways to tell them that something was wrong. They seemed to understand from the expressions on his face and his persistence that what he needed to say was quite important. His indifference to the food that they brought seemed to confirm this. In his efforts, he learnt that the second Alien's name was Gadin. Try as he might Xander was not able to get through to them. They finally gave up and started to leave for the main level. Xander did not. He tried to follow them. At first they motioned to him to stay and Bodak pulled out a weapon again. Xander reflexly winced. Gadin said something rapidly to Bodak. Then to Xander's surprise, Bodak motioned him to follow them.

This he did down the narrow stairway with some difficulty as he still had those magnetic restraints. Xander barely recognized the main level of the Pelican 25. There had been numerous changes to it. Different equipment, computers and additions to the Pelican 25 systems were everywhere. Xander walked towards the main computer controls. He was hoping he could show them what the problem was. Bodak quickly motioned him away with a stern look whilst waving his weapon at him. Xander hurriedly stepped away. He realized that it was in his interest not to incite his captors. It would not take much provocation for them to eliminate him. He was well aware of the fact that he was using up limited resources and space on the ship. In what was a potentially long and taxing trip.

Xander looked around. More slowly this time. In a small room to his right, with its doors opened, something caught his eye. Lying on a table or a bed without pillows was another Alien. He was immobile and looked dead from this distance. Xander did not see any movement of his chest to indicate breathing. But there was a device like large headphones attached to head, just above his ears. None of this made any sense to him.

Bodak called another name loudly. Sounded like Hadik. Another Alien appeared. He must have been sleeping as his eyes seemed bleary. Both Gadin and Bodak spoke to him quickly. He nodded and started following what seemed like instructions. He got a large piece of equipment out of a box and set it out on a table. He fiddled with a few buttons and lights came on. He smiled and looked up to the others. They spoke to him again. Then they motioned for him to sit down. Xander complied. Hadik took a small microphone attached to the machine and placed it near Xander's mouth. Hadik seemed curiously enthusiastic.

Xander smiled. He was almost certain he knew what this was. He had seen versions of it before. It was a language machine of some sort. He would speak in his language and the machine would convert it to the Alien language and vice versa.

He spoke slowly and clearly.

"My name is Xander."

"I am aboard the Pelican 25 spaceship. We are traveling too fast."

He paused.

"My home system is Earth. We were visiting the Ixodia system and its moons Aqualon and Riad."

He paused again. Nothing happened. A few crackles from the machine. That was all. He was beginning to doubt that this would work. No further sound from the machine. Perhaps his language was not represented in their database.

Hadik picked up another microphone and spoke rapidly into the machine. Still no response from the machine. He motioned to Xander to start speaking again. Xander patiently continued.

"My father is an astronomer. I wish to return to Aqualon. I wish to return to my family and friends."

He paused. And after a few more anxious moments, audio output from the language machine began. It seemed to translate some of what he said to them. But the audio output was in their language only. Hadik smiled and nodded. They could now communicate. Even if it was a slow process and perhaps not very accurate, they had a method. Even Bodak nodded. Xander knew he must now try to get his message across, in a one way language machine. He had no way of knowing what words the machine could decipher accurately, much less context. He had to take his chances.

"We are traveling too fast," Xander repeated slowly.

"The ship will crash." He repeated his message with varied language to give the machine some alternate words to convey his message.

"Very dangerous to go at this speed," he continued slowly and earnestly.

It was slow going and very tedious but Xander persisted.

II.

Mondeus relayed the events of the night before to Jelina. It took some time and a lot of effort. Jelina listened without interrupting. When Mondeus got to the part of Xander getting shot, she flinched visibly. Mondeus was almost hysterical and it was torture just to have him recall the events. They had stayed out of earshot of Arielle but it did not seem to matter any more. Arielle was critically ill. They did not know whether Xander was alive. Their major avenue for getting help had failed. And their ship was probably gone as Mondeus had recalled hearing engine noise consistent with take off during his frantic flight.

Finally Jelina mustered the courage to ask "Did they take Xander on the ship?" Mondeus shook his head. He did not know for sure. In panic he had fled before he could witness the ship's departure. He had thought that they would shoot him too if they had seen him.

Jelina's next words were coldly sobering.

"We must return to the Alien's cavern," she said slowly and deliberately.

Mondeus stared at her with wide, frightened eyes. He knew she was dead serious. He did not speak.

"Xander could still be there and wounded," she continued, even more slowly.

As afraid as Mondeus was, he realized that she was right. They had to return.

"And Arielle?" he asked.

"We will have to take the risk and leave her here. For a while anyway," Jelina said. She was sounding more like Xander with each passing minute.

Jelina was well aware of how exhausted Mondeus must be. He had very little rest and goodness knows how many miles he had covered on foot when he got lost. All he had had was water and the last scraps of food they had remaining. Let alone the trauma of the events he had witnessed. And she was asking him to go trekking for a few more miles. His adrenaline was waning now. Even fear could not keep it that elevated for so long.

Still, time was of the essence. They must try to get to the cave and return before dark. Because it was already afternoon, that did not seem likely. But if they set out immediately, they should be able to get to the landing site with enough light to look around. Maybe the Aliens left Xander in their cave.

Jelina walked over to Arielle, who was lying propped up at about 30 degrees in a corner of their current abode. She told Arielle what they were going to do. Arielle appeared to be slipping into a deeper coma and Jelina doubted that Arielle heard a word of what she said. Yet like the dutiful sister she was, Jelina explained in detail what their plans were. It pained

Jelina to leave Arielle alone, injured and critically ill. What if she awoke and didn't see them? How would she know that they did not abandon her?

Jelina had considered going to the cave by herself so Mondeus could stay with Arielle. However, she decided to have Mondeus accompany her as she would need help if they found Xander. Jelina knew that they had no choice. Images of a wounded Xander, lying waiting for help kept flashing through her mind. Jelina touched Arielle face tenderly and said goodbye. With heavy hearts, they set off on the trip back to the landing site and into the unknown.

III.

Arielle awoke suddenly to the rumbling of thunder. It was louder than normal. It seemed to be coming from very close, in the far corner of the cave. She tried to clear the fog from her brain. But it wouldn't go away. Her eyelids were heavy. She wondered why thunder often seemed so close but lightning was always so far away. The sudden thunder startled her again. No, this wasn't thunder. She felt a few pebbles falling on her leg and dust in her face. A jolt of panic went through her. In that brief moment, there was some clarity. This was some kind of an earthquake. And she was trapped in a large cave!

She tried to call out to Xander. And Jelina. First, there was no sound coming from her mouth. And then a hoarse croaking voice that she did not recognize as her own, came from her lips.

"Xander."

"Jelina."

"Mondeus," she cried. In vain.

"Help."

"Help me."

"HELP!"

No answer. In panic, she tried to think. She could not move. Her right leg was very heavy. And it would not obey her. She recalled bits and pieces now. She was ill. Something was wrong with her leg. She was in a cave. And there was some kind of tremors or earthquake taking place. She must get out of the cave. Quickly.

"Xander."

"Jelina!" she tried again. Her voice was terse. But it was barely more than a whisper.

Where are they? she thought. *Why did they leave me alone?*

She was tired. And wanted to go back to sleep. Forget about the deep rumbling and just go back to sleep. And then the noise started again. Almost above her. She could hear the rocks falling in the cave very close to her. And felt dust all over her. Her will returned a bit stronger now. She had to do something. Somewhere in the recesses of her mind, she remembered Jelina saying that they were going back to the landing site.

Was it Jelina or Xander? She remembered it sounded like Jelina. When was that? Was it yesterday? What time was it? Was it day or night? It was completely dark. It must be night then. How long had she been here alone?

She had no way of telling. Her hours and days were indistinguishable. Why did they abandon her? Did they abandon her? No, it couldn't be. Her friends would not leave her alone to die. There must be some reason for this. They must have gone to get help.

The rumbling would not let her thoughts flow. It started again. She groped around her. And felt something. It was a flashlight. Jelina must have left it there. With effort, she put it on and moved it around. Finally, some luck. She was much more awake now. The light seemed to have activated some areas of her brain. She must get out of the cave. It could collapse anytime now. And bury her without leaving a trace. She was glad she found the light. As she moved it around, she saw some of their equipment lying nearby. She saw her leg in a splint. Swollen and red. Most importantly she saw the mouth of the cave. It was in the *opposite* direction in which she had thought. If she had started moving without this light, she would have gone further into the cave.

She made up her mind. She would not give up. With a Herculean effort she started dragging her body. With her injured leg trailing. Inch by inch she moved. The gravel bruised her left arm. Took the skin off her left elbow. As she used her arm opposite her wounded leg for traction. Several times she collapsed flat on the ground. And wanted to give up. But the continued rumbling made her stay alert. And compelled her to keep going.

As she approached the mouth of the cave, she saw the faint light from outside. She was getting close. It encouraged her. But there was also a slight upslope to the entrance. She was exhausted from her efforts. So close, and yet so far away. She must continue. Arielle saw the face of Xander. Smiling. Ever so calming. And it motivated her to continue. Uphill. A small slope that seemed like a steep mountain now. Dragging her body. Inch by inch. Using all her willpower and mental fortitude. Some of which she did not even know existed. Closer and closer. To the mouth of the cave, she edged. As the deep rumblings continued.

IV.

Bodak, Hadik and Gadin exchanged looks.

Xander continued, "We're traveling too fast!"

They seem to understand the essence of what he was saying. Another excited chattering broke out among them again.

Xander noticed that Bodak was shaking his head firmly in disagreement.

Hadik asked Xander something. Xander now had a blank expression. He did not understand a word.

Hadik tried again. This time Hadik spoke into the microphone of the language device. He spoke several sentences without waiting for an output. It seemed as if he was calibrating it in some way. Finally he stopped.

After what seemed like a long time of waiting, it crackled to life again. And started responding slowly.

"Cooorrreeect."

Xander managed to interpret that as "correct". Yet he was confused. They did not seem to agree with him, yet they were telling him, or rather the machine was translating "correct."

The device continued "no, agree."

They knew, by the look on his face, that Xander was perplexed.

"No, correct."

And then Xander realized what they were saying. They knew he understood too by his sudden expression of comprehension. It was there for all to see.

They were saying that "He was NOT correct." They either did not agree with him or did not believe him. And he saw them shaking their heads.

Xander became bolder. He walked over to the main controlling computer, towards the center of the room. This time they did not stop him but followed with interest. He pointed to the panels of instruments on the screen. He isolated the one for speed and again showed that this was too high. They understood by nodding their heads. But they did nothing. They either did not believe him or thought he had some ulterior motive for wishing to go at less than maximum speed.

Xander hung his head in disappointment. Then despair. He did manage to get his message through. But he failed to get anyone to act on it. He was in the same position as he was just hours ago. One thing he knew for sure, the ship would not last too long at this rate. How long was too long? He did not know for sure. And then another thought crossed his mind. The Aliens did modify the ship considerably in the short time they had. Could they have modified the engine to tolerate such speeds? His moment of hope quickly faded. Even if they did, the actual body and structure of the Pelican 25 was not constructed to sustain these speeds for any length of time. One way or another, they were doomed; heading for disaster.

* * * * *

Jelina was quiet for a while. Her mind was racing. That their situation was dire was a gross understatement. She tried to keep her focus on Xander and hoped that somehow he was alive. Alive and in the cavern next to the landing site. The one the Aliens had used when they stole their ship. She refused to consider that he was dead. Refused to consider that the Aliens took Xander with them. She figured that if he was, was...dead, they would not. Jelina pushed that line of thought out her mind again. At the moment, she had to be the strongest in their group. Arielle was critically ill. Mondeus was not at all himself. No surprise after what he had gone through. She must try to think clearly.

They were out of food now. Nothing to eat. They would have to start chancing the plant life. And hope that their random choices were non toxic. She tried to go faster. Mondeus could not keep up. She held his hands and tried to tow him along. That made little difference. She was afraid that he would collapse. That would mean that they would not get there before dark. And a night in the cold, under the elements was not an appealing thought. She finally left him to plod along at his own pace. Mondeus was too tired to speak. He drank water repeatedly from the flask that they had brought along. And they kept going.

The suns were low in the sky as they approached the original landing site of the Pelican 25. The one they landed on what seemed to be a lifetime ago. Good. They should be able to find the cavern without too much trouble. Mondeus walked straight to the corner where the cavern was located. They need not worry. The Aliens did not even bother to close the doorway to the cavern. There was a huge gaping hole at the side of the hill. The steepest hill bordering the clearing. *How had we missed this before?* Jelina thought. It seemed too large to miss. But Jelina noticed that it was cleverly concealed. Vegetation growing over the large, retractable doorway was the main reason.

Jelina was sure that all the Aliens were gone. But it was not an absolute certainty. With great apprehension they approached the entrance of the cavern. With greater apprehension, Mondeus stayed in tow. He was afraid to go in. But he could not let Jelina do it alone. So with wooden legs he followed, holding on to her arm. Jelina paused at the doorway and then crossed over the threshold. She and Mondeus walked a few steps and suddenly they were in a huge cathedral like space. They put their flashlights on high, and gaped. They moved the flashlights around 360 degrees and their jaws dropped in utter amazement. This changed to incredulity, then bewilderment as they digested their surroundings.

They were in a huge cavern. With a high roof of what appeared to be hewn rock. The size of this thing was astonishing. And a lot of it seemed to have been man-made. Even more shocking were the contents around them. A spaceship! Larger than theirs. With large parts of it scattered around the cavern. Separated from the main structure. As if it was taken apart. Or in the process of being repaired.

Signs that this place was inhabited were everywhere. And it was clear that it was home for a number of people. For a long time as well. Tables. Chairs. Beds. It was too much to take in all at once. They saw many small enclosures with low lying walls. They appeared to be rooms without doors. A very large central area. With wide connecting passageways. One led to another large section in the back. Most of that area seemed to have been carved out of the rock. But there were no signs of anyone being home right now.

Jelina tried to overcome her shock. She must remain composed, she told herself. And remember their primary goal. Find Xander. They began to look around methodically searching for him. Ignoring pretty much everything else that surrounded them. They called out to him.

"Xander."

"Xander!"

Their voices had strange echoes in this large cavern. No answer.

They looked and looked. No Xander.

They started from the beginning again. Went into every enclosure they could identify. In every corner, they looked. No luck. They moved to the farthest area of the cave. Furthest away from the entrance. They discovered a back entrance to the cave. Or was that an exit? It looked like any of the other corridors. But there was light coming from it. And it did not lead to a dead end, like the others. It led directly to the other side of the hill, under which this vast structure was located. The hill which was pretty innocuous looking from the clearing, was much bigger than they had previously thought. They looked and looked. Still no evidence of Xander.

Finally they sat down. On the chairs that the Aliens used. To collect their thoughts. Jelina broke the silence.

"I think we can be quite sure that Xander is not here," she said slowly.

Mondeus nodded his head in agreement.

In some strange way, this gave Jelina hope.

"If the Aliens took him, I am sure he is still alive," she continued.

"They would not have done that otherwise," she explained to Mondeus.

"That makes sense," Mondeus said with some hope. For the first time in a long time, she saw a flicker of positive emotion in his eyes.

They had surmised a lot from their exploration.

"It looks like several people lived this cave. For a long time too," Jelina noted.

"It could have been years," Mondeus pointed out.

"It appeared as if they were stranded here. Probably from the malfunctioning spaceship," he deduced. It was Jelina's turn to nod in agreement.

They could not be sure. It was an educated guess, looking at the parts of the spaceship strewn around them. They had expanded the cave and constructed various sections of it to live in. There were wires, lighting systems and many other power driven devices including heating systems. There were sleeping areas, beds and the equivalent of bedrooms. There was a cooking area, food and all the things one would associated with a small group of people inhabiting a place for an extended period of time.

Whoever lived here was not at all primitive. As Mondeus and Jelina surveyed the main body of the spaceship, Mondeus figured that these Aliens were quite advanced. Probably even more technologically advanced than they themselves were. Mondeus could not understand a lot of their systems. Other than turning on lights and basic devices, he had no clue of how their systems worked or were powered. With some time he thought he may be able to figure some of it out. Time was in short supply at the moment. And he was too tired to concentrate.

By now, it had gotten completely dark outside of the cave. Jelina was debating whether they would have to stay here overnight or try to return to their cave. She hoped and prayed that Arielle would be all right. There were lots of things that they could use from here. Food and water were in adequate supply. It was warm here too. She was also sure that given time, Mondeus could figure out a way to power up their own mobile communicating devices again.

It was while she was contemplating this that the rumbling began. And the tremors. Mondeus recognized them immediately. He had experienced several small earthquakes during his childhood. Jelina knew too, even though she was a Voyager. And their minds immediately went to Arielle. All alone, and deep underground in a cave. One very much unlike the structure that were sitting in now. One that had no reinforced roof nor walls. And she was unable to move. A new round of panic entered their brains.

"We have to get back to her," Jelina cried out aloud, as she leapt to her feet.

"Let's go," Mondeus said worriedly, as the tremors got stronger and stronger.

V.

They found her as soon as they got there. The tremors had long stopped. It had taken them several hours and more than a few missteps to get back to the cave. It was cold and dark. And they would have never found it if it were not for Mondeus's mistakes the night before. But he had learnt well. Even under the weight of tiredness and exhaustion, he managed to use the hills and the skyline to navigate them back to the cave. It was not a direct route as they would have done in the day. But it was never too far off course.

They were not sure if she was alive when they reached her. She was just outside the mouth of the cave.

"Arielle!" Jelina called out in a hoarse voice.

"Arielle," Mondeus implored with a cracked voice, higher pitched than usual.

No answer.

"ARIELLE!" Jelina screamed.

"Arielle," wailed Mondeus.

Still no answer.

"Oh no," Jelina cried, just about losing all control now.

"We have to help her," Mondeus said as he rushed to kneel by her side.

Arielle did make it out of their cave. Most of it collapsed soon after. Sections of the entire roof caved in. She was not aware of that. All she knew was that she was lying outside of the opening and looking up at the stars. She also felt cold and remembered starting to shiver. She had no protection, except the clothes she had on. And then she slipped into darkness once again.

"Oh my god!" Jelina cried as she knelt to the other side of Arielle.

They saw she was badly bruised and her clothes were in tatters. Jelina's hand went to her pulse.

At the same time, Mondeus cried, "She is alive!"

He thought he saw her chest move with a shallow breath.

Jelina also felt a pulse. A weak one and she rested her head on Arielle's chest to put her own fears at rest. She heard Arielle's heart sounds, beating rapidly.

"What are we going to do now?" Mondeus asked looking at Jelina.

For the moment they forgot all about Xander. They had to think about surviving the rest of the night. Arielle appeared to be in a deep sleep once more, or more correctly, in a comatose state.

Mondeus and Jelina peered into their cave with their flashlights. To their horror, they saw most of the roof had fallen in. There was rubble all around. They wanted to get the sleeping units and get Arielle warm. Also to retrieve whatever was remaining of their few supply items. It was all buried under tons of rocks and dirt. There was barely any way to get in. Let alone accessing in the rear areas of the cave. Not possible. In despair, Mondeus moaned "How awful!"

Jelina shook her head with a semblance of thought returning.

"No. It is a miracle. She got out. In time."

That sort of put their buried items in perspective.

"Yes, it is," he said slowly.

They moved closer to Arielle. Her fate almost seemed out of their hands now. But they would do as much as humanly possible to help her.

"We will move to the Alien's cave. There are lots of supplies and food there," Jelina said quietly.

Mondeus nodded. That part was fairly obvious.

Jelina was silent for a while. They were both getting colder. Jelina had already taken her extra sweater off and covered Arielle with it. It could not be nearly enough for her in her condition.

Finally Mondeus said, "Arielle?"

It was what they were both thinking.

Another pause.

And then Jelina said, more confidently than she was feeling,

"We will take her."

Mondeus refrained from asking his usual "How?"

He remembered the difficulty they had in getting her here. And that was with Xander shouldering most of the work. And now, she was ten times more ill.

He nodded and quietly said "OK."

A slight wind reminded them that they were entirely under the elements. It seemed even colder now that they were not moving. Mondeus and Jelina briefly discussed going back in the still intact area of the cave for shelter. They decided against it. It was too risky. There could be aftershocks and a total collapse would trap them all inside. They will have to take their chances here. It was still a few hours to daylight. And warmth. It would become colder yet before the suns rose. Such was the nature of sandy moons.

They had to keep Arielle as warm as they could. Jelina took off some more of her clothing and covered Arielle. Any extra layering would help. She took heart from the fact, that when she moved Arielle's infected leg, some sound escaped her lips. It must have caused some deep pain. But in a strange kind of way it comforted Jelina that Arielle was still with them.

Mondeus suggested that they move her just a few meters away to the other side of the cave. Where they were protected from the wind. This helped but it not easy to carry an immobile Arielle for even a short distance. Jelina laid down next to Arielle and like the good sister she was, pressed her body against Arielle to provide whatever warmth she could. Mondeus found some dried leaves and heaped it over their legs and rested on the other side of Arielle. There they were, huddled, waiting for the suns to come up. Or for some miracle to save them.

VI.

There was only faint light on the outside of the Pelican 25. Xander was quickly losing track of how long he had been on board the ship. His ship. For starters, he was not sure how long he had been unconscious. He imagined that they were some distance from Aqualon and perhaps even out of the Ixodia system by now. One thing he was certain about, the Pelican 25 was remarkably well built. It had withstood the extraordinary speeds they were traveling at. It was hard for him to think whilst feeling that he was sitting on a time bomb. Perhaps the Aliens had installed some sort of buffers and dampeners to make this speed manageable. He could only hope. He was aware of the significant changes that were made to the controls of the ship. That was probably the reason why the Aliens had not immediately taken off in the stolen ship.

Xander also observed that the Aliens slept a lot. Only two or three were awake at any one time. So far he had counted six plus the one who seemed to be in a coma with the device attached to his head. He had made up his mind.

"Hadik," Xander called.

Hadik came over and look questioningly at him. Xander motioned at the translating machine. Hadik turned it on after a moment's hesitation. Hadik realized that Xander wanted to talk. Hadik was also curious and seemed interested in communicating with him.

At first it was painfully slow. As the machine adapted, it improved. Xander could almost carry on a conversation with Hadik, as the machine now interpreted both their native languages. What Xander learnt was utterly amazing. It was worth the effort and more.

The Aliens were a people called the Gadorans. They were from an entirely different system, not at all close to Ixodia. In fact, they were from a part of the galaxy quite a distance away. They did not know where they were for a long time. Bodak and his men were the crew of a cargo ship. It was involved in a freak accident in which they were hit by some space debris. It had happened during an intense electrical storm that rendered their navigational instruments useless. They had sustained major damage to their ship and had lost all communication capabilities. They had flown around blindly for weeks. Eventually they crash landed on Riad. They did not know the name of the moon. Hadik explained that they were initially overjoyed to find that it was habitable. And had a nontoxic atmosphere.

That was in the beginning. Two of their men were injured in the accident. They had badly needed medical attention. They both died within the first few months on the moon. As amazing as his story was, Xander's jaw dropped open when Hadik told him that this was almost *thirty years ago*. Xander had him repeat it just to make sure that it was translated correctly.

Hadik was a scientist of some sort and appear to derive satisfaction from knowledge and the things that Xander told him. That they were on Riad, a moon in the Ixodia system. Hadik had heard of the Ixodia system but did not have any detailed knowledge of it. He had never heard of Riad. They had long suspected they were in that system by their survey of the surrounding stars and planetary systems. They had managed to salvage a few instruments from their damaged spaceship. But they were only able to confirm their exact location a few days ago. They had used the intact systems of the Pelican 25 to do so. It was essential as they needed to chart a route back to their home world from this starting point.

"How did you survive for so long?" Xander asked.

Hadik continued patiently, eager for the opportunity to tell someone their story.

There were twelve crew members on the Gadoran's cargo ship initially. They were carrying a full shipment, mainly food and some other supplies to a planet some distance away. They were traders for their planet, in a sense. They had made this run a few times before. And were well equipped for long journeys. They had hit the storm in the last week of their trip. That is when they were blown completely off course. To nowhere they knew.

After they crash landed on Riad, their main goals were to get help for their injured crew members. And to get rescued. They soon realized that whilst the moon was habitable, it was uninhabited by humans, as far as they could tell. They had no way of reaching anyone. After they lost the first two of the crew, they made some long term plans for survival and to increase their chances of being rescued.

The Gadorans hopes were high in the first few months. They had heard sounds and seen lights that were compatible with ships close to the planet. So they knew visitors came to Raid occasionally. In the first few weeks they were there, they had thought that it was just a matter of time before they would get help. A craft had landed some miles from where the Gadorans cavern was. They had seen its lights and heard it. They ran for many miles to the site. It was much further than they thought. Just before they reached the vicinity the craft departed. Yet, it left them hopeful.

But the weeks soon turned into months. They scouted some of the moon. Used telescopic glasses from the hilltops to look for inhabitants, buildings, anything that would lead them to help. A few months later, they thought that they had another chance. It was during the daylight hours. And it was close by. They could clearly hear the engines of the spacecraft. They all ran rapidly to the site.

As they all reached there, they shouted and waved their hands. They were almost certain they were seen. But inexplicably, the spacecraft took off leaving them standing there. Dejected and despondent. Their hopes dashed. They stood there for a long time. And finally they had to make the long walk back to their cavern. Trying to keep their hopes alive.

In the meantime, they made the cavern their home. They enlarged it. Brought their spaceship into it. Tried everything in their power to repair it. Numerous attempts but, alas, all unsuccessful. It was too badly damaged. They eventually used some of its power systems to produce heat and light. In the beginning, food was not a problem as they used the supplies from the ship. But with each passing week, they knew they did not have an indefinite supply.

It was several years later before they got another opportunity to be rescued.

* * * * *

An older Gadoran named Hodan was the commander of their ship. His deputy was the younger Bodak who only became the leader after Hodan died. Hodan was less authoritative and wiser than Bodak. He had planned and carefully so. He worked out that the greatest chance of him and his crew ever getting rescued was to increase the likelihood of a chance encounter with visitors to the moon. In the meantime, they had to stay alive and make the best use of the limited resources they had.

The Gadorans were a people who grew to height of between five and five and one half feet. But they easily lived more than one hundred years. Partly because they could spend long periods in a trance like sleep or a form of hibernation, which slowed their aging process. They could reduce their metabolism, heart rate, breathing etc. to well below fifty per cent of their norm. Hodan had given instructions that they would go into hibernation for about twenty eight of every thirty days. There were long debates of whether they needed to all hibernate together or wake up sequentially. The wise Hodan recommended that they were up two at a time, sequentially. That would increase the number of days that a person would be awake and hence increase their chance of finding some help. That was to change in the latter years but this was how plans went into effect at the time.

The translator was working overtime. However, it was learning from the additional input and kept adapting. It was working at quite a reasonable pace now.

"What happened to Hodan?" asked Xander.

"He was killed trying to get help," Hadik said slowly.

Xander dropped his eyes but Hadik shook his head understandingly.

"At first the plan was for the two Gadorans awake to rouse all of us if they saw any ships. We had a couple of false alarms with ships passing overhead. Hodan then decided that unless we actually saw other humans landing, the others should remain asleep."

"You see this interfered with our metabolism. To be roused suddenly during hibernation caused ill effects. We needed to go down for about four weeks at a time. Some of us had done this before during long travel with the cargo ship. It wasn't too difficult."

"Hodan also mapped out duties for all of us. We had a strict calendar of work. After we made enough living space for all of us, he divided the duties based on our skills and training. Each Gadoran performed their task with pride as all of our lives depended on it. Because of the schedule we did not meet each other awake for long periods. Hodan knew that we needed to talk and that was one reason he had us waking up in two's, even though we could have had more waking days if only one of us was up at a time."

"Who was your partner?" Xander asked hoping to continue the conversation.

Hadik did not need any prompting.

"My waking partner's name was Jedan. He was the chief technical person on our ship. A very learned Gadoran. He tried with all his life to fix our ship. For too long, perhaps. He finally gave up after Hodan recommended that he did. He felt as if he had let us all down but most of us already knew that our ship was never going to fly again. It was only then that he dismantled the ship systems. We used some of the parts to power heating and lighting in our makeshift home. It made us more comfortable at the time."

"Where is he now?" Xander prompted. No sooner had he asked this question, he wished he hadn't. Hadik's eyes became misty and he looked away.

But after a moment, he continued "Jedan did not wake up one day."

"About five years ago, we went back to sleep after waking Gadin and his partner. Jedan was tired as he had worked very hard during the time we were up. When I woke up for our next work shift, I was the only one to get up. He had died in his sleep."

The tears were apparent in his eyes now and Hadik made no attempt to conceal them.

"I did not bother to wake the others. So, I had to put him away myself."

Xander assumed that meant burying or whatever means the Gadorans used to dispose of the body.

"His hope was to see his family again. And that is why he kept working so hard. His body could not take more after so long. It just could not revive itself any longer."

"I am sorry to hear that," Xander muttered rather awkwardly.

Xander did not have the heart to ask Hadik to keep going. Hadik shook his head and kept on after a few moments of silence. He wanted to tell someone their story. It was as if he were afraid it could be lost forever. They must have felt so on countless occasions. There was a lot that was still unclear to Xander but he did not want to ask directly. However, as Hadik's story continued, Xander began to understand much more of the Gadoran's plight.

As if reading his mind, Hadik gestured towards the room with the Gadoran who appeared comatose.

"He is very ill. He is getting some treatment now. We are trying to keep him alive until we can get him medical attention. We did not have a doctor on board the ship. A few of us had basic medical training but there was not very much we could do on that moon."

"We started with twelve on the crew. We lost two of our brothers soon after the accident. Hodan died about twelve years later. Then a few years ago, my friend Jedan died. We are now seven plus one Gadoran who is on his last breath."

Xander felt great sadness for the Gadorans. It was quiet in the ship now and for a moment, Xander forgot about the dangerous speed they were traveling at. Even in his befuddled state, he noticed that Hadik did not elaborate on Hodan. Hadik had said earlier that Hodan was killed. Perhaps there was some internal battle for their leadership? He would ask later. Hadik became silent again. Xander's mind drifted back to Riad. And to Mondeus and Jelina and Arielle. With what he just heard from Hadik, he was afraid to even think of what could become of them. And being trapped here on a ship, going to some unknown part of the galaxy, he could not help them. He also refused to think of his own fate.

VII.

The suns slipped over the horizon on Riad. The light woke Mondeus. He was surprised that he had fallen asleep. It seemed colder this morning than before. It was not. It was just because they were completely under the elements. There were no further rumblings. It was very still and it appeared as if the tremors of the night before had never taken place.

Mondeus looked over at Jelina. And Arielle. Jelina's eyes were closed. She was huddled into Arielle. With some relief, he saw Arielle's chest moving slowly. Breathing.

"Jelie," he called softly.

"Jelie, wake up!" he said more intensely, still under hushed tones.

Jelina opened her eyes. And for a fleeting second, Mondeus saw the look in her eyes. It was one of worry and despair and pain. All at the same time.

She and Mondeus got up. How quickly it got warmer on this moon! Both suns were in full view now. Heat, not cold, would be a factor in their trip. Mondeus and Jelina both had a determined look in their eyes. They knew it was going to be a very, very, long day. But they would do it. The Gadorans cavern had food and water. And heat and light. They just had to get there. And get there, they would. Carrying their own with them. It was going to be some journey. A long journey. With as many stops as needed. But they will get there eventually.

* * * * *

Hadik and one other Gadoran was awake. Xander had developed some human bond with Hadik. Xander wondered if he told Hadik their story, if he could convince him to turn the ship around and return to Riad. He somehow doubted that. He was not sure that even if Hadik wanted to, Bodak would allow it. Xander did not know how far away from Raid they were. Traveling at this speed, it must be quite a distance already. He could map it out if he were allowed to use the instruments and controls of the

Pelican 25. The Gadorans did not allow him to get close in his last attempt. And he remembered that it was just less than two days ago, he was shot by Bodak. And essentially kidnapped. Or was it just about two days ago?

Xander took a gamble and chose what he hoped was a diplomatic approach.

"How did Hodan die?" he asked rather bravely.

Hadik looked at him strangely. This time he appeared as if he was not going to answer. After a long pause, Hadik said, "He was killed."

Xander waited. Hadik did not elaborate.

After a much longer pause, with some harshness in his tone, Hadik stated "He was killed trying to get help."

"We were stranded there for about twelve years, when one day there were visitors. They landed in the exact spot you landed. That was the same clearing where we had crash landed many years before. It was a long wait, but it did not seem like so many years. Remember, we were only awake for about 4 weeks of each year. So the time passed relatively quickly. Hodan and Jedan were the ones out of hibernation when these visitors came. Jedan was his partner at the time. We believe that twice during our sleep before this, visitors came and went. And we missed them."

"Hodan was later able to tell us, how overjoyed and excited, he was. He and Jedan ran out of the cave immediately and called out to the visitors. They did not understand a word that the Gadorans spoke. They seemed very surprised and were clearly upset that they were disturbed by the Gadorans. They didn't seem to want to have company. Perhaps they were smugglers or criminals of some kind, Hodan later suggested. At any rate, Hodan knew that shady or not, this was an opportunity that they could not miss out on. Hodan and Jedan ran towards the ship, hailing the visiting ship. They were fired upon. With destructive weapons. Jedan was injured but not as badly as Hodan. Jedan brought Hodan back to our cave dwelling. He roused us all. By now, the visiting ship had left. Hodan was able to tell us what took place. But he died a few days later. Jedan recovered with time."

Xander was a good listener. He thought Hadik was finished. He was wrong. Hadik looked around carefully. Bodak and the other Gadorans had retired to rest. The only other Gadoran awake was at the upper level, in what used to be Xander's quarters.

"After Hodan died, we had an extremely difficult period. Hodan was a close friend, you see. He had wanted me to take over the leadership role if he were no longer capable. We had known each for many years prior to the accident. And we had made quite a few trips together before. Bodak is much younger than I am. But he was the appointed deputy on that fateful trip, when we crashed. As such, he insisted that he should become the leader. Most of the Gadorans did not agree with him. They wanted me to take charge. I saw that there was going to be trouble amongst us if Bodak did not become the leader. He was younger and more aggressive. Also very impatient. After a few days of long debates and heated disagreements, I decided to change stance. I then recommended him to be the leader. The other Gadorans reluctantly agreed. I knew we couldn't afford incessant conflict. It would have been destructive in a closed group like us. We needed to be united to survive."

"As soon as Bodak became leader, he changed all the rules. He instructed that we all slept and woke up at the same time period. He commanded that if any vessel landed, we were to take it by use of force and weapons. Because we were up for only about two to three days every month, we had to work very hard to keep our survival measures in place. Bodak made us go by foot as far as possible and spend nights camping in the open, so we could cover as much land as possible looking for any random visitors. After this brought no success in the next few cycles, he doubled our waking time and made us go even further."

"This was taking a toll on us. We were getting weaker and aging much quicker now that we were staying up more. We were also using more food and supplies. This continued for several years. But it was clear to us that we missed at least six ships landing in close proximity to us, when we were all sleeping. After much discussion, we finally managed to persuade Bodak to go back to the method Hodan had used. Bodak was from a military background and didn't take too well to recommendations. He wanted to use force and strength to overcome everything. Reasoning is not his strongest asset."

Xander could vividly imagine the years of hope and disappointment that the Gadorans must have experienced. The futility that came when months grew into years and then decades. He also felt that Hadik was giving him some hint on the character of Bodak. Essentially telling him that Bodak would not compromise nor reason with Xander. Xander knew as far as Bodak was concerned, he was lucky to be alive.

It seemed as if all that Hadik wanted to say for now, he had said.

Xander decided to return to the present. He asked again, knowing that he couldn't be misunderstood now.

"Did you modify this ship to travel faster?"

Hadik nodded. "It was one of the reasons we took so long to leave. We boosted the engines, using some technology from our old ship."

"But the body of this ship cannot take such speeds," Xander weakly protested.

Hadik smiled warmly at him, almost like an understanding father

"We used electrical power to add a kind of shield. It would dampen the effects of the increased speed."

Xander could not dispute this. The Gadorans seemed to have made more advances in space travel than humans from the System. With a thin smile Hadik added, "It was our only hope to get back to our home system. We think it may work even though there is no way to be sure."

Xander relaxed somewhat with this news.

Hadik nodded to him. "Get some rest. My turn to keep watch will soon be over."

Xander realized that the other Gadorans may not be quite as understanding as Hadik.

VIII.

The trip to the Gadorans' dwelling was a hundred times harder than when they first carried a hurt but very conscious Arielle. For many reasons too. The most obvious being there was no Xander this time. Arielle being dead weight was another huge factor. They were already exhausted after a few hundred meters. The heat from the suns quickly sapped the energy from Mondeus and Jelina.

For the umpteenth time, it crossed Jelina's mind that they would not make it. Or if they did, it would be too late for Arielle. They were too tired to talk. But Jelina still made efforts to encourage Mondeus and some things were in their favor.

"We don't have any packs to carry," she panted, referring to the first trip when they carried their supplies as well Arielle. There was barely any acknowledgement from Mondeus.

"And we don't have to worry about getting lost," she reminded him, comparing their trip to the last time yet again. Mondeus nodded this time.

Perhaps Jelina was making these remarks to allay her own fears. Even so, she was sure Mondeus shared those fears.

They had learnt from the last time too. Before they had started, they knew they had to make a sort of stretcher. They used Mondeus's shirt and Jelina's sweater. They cut the fabric into strips. Mondeus found two poles of what seemed like strong enough wood and joined them together with the fabric. They hoped that this would be strong enough to carry their patient. Finding large enough poles was not an easy task on this moon without any big trees. But the one they eventually settled on seemed to be able to carry the weight of Arielle comfortably.

After what seemed to be their fiftieth stop in the last couple of hours, Jelina suggested that they rest for a little longer. More than the couple of minutes that they had been using to catch their breath. As they sat down, they noticed that Arielle seemed to have opened her eyes. Just for the briefest of moments. But enough to encourage them. This spurred them on with renewed vigor.

Time and again they stopped to rest. Take fifty steps they told themselves. Then stop and catch a breath. Take fifty more and so on. Time and again they thought that they would not make it. And they wouldn't have. Except for one simple fact. The fact that the last half of a mile or so of their trip was sloped downwards. Not a big slope. But enough to make a vast difference in this journey. If fate had had it that this was an upslope, they were pretty certain that they would not have made it back to the Gadorans cave with Arielle alive. They had long passed the point of exhaustion.

* * * * *

Xander must have fallen asleep in the main cabin. Hadik was kind enough to remove the magnetic handcuffs from him. And he was able to stretch out and relax. Hadik seemed to believe that Xander was not dangerous. They had given him food him again. In fact, the Gadorans were treating him reasonably well. Except for the little matter of them taking him to some unknown part of the galaxy. Where he may never see his own people again. Or ever return to his family and friends.

Xander saw Bodak briefly. He barely paid any attention to Xander. He grumbled something to the other Gadorans. Sounded like some type of order or instruction. Or an update of some sort. He then went promptly back to his quarters and out of sight. Xander deduced that Bodak was not the most popular of the Gadorans. He was sure that Hadik could not cover all the events that took place in the last thirty years with Bodak.

Bodak appeared to be using the lower level of the Pelican 25 for his base. Xander surmised that their journey was preset and pretty much controlled by the ship computers. The Gadorans must have bridged their instruments to the Pelican 25 systems. Most of the time, only one or two Gadorans were at the main level. They kept to their own quarters. That is, if they were awake at all. Gadin was there currently. He was the Gadoran that Xander first met on the ship. With Bodak.

Xander did not know whether it was day or night. And it did not really matter as they must be a long way from the Suns in the Ixodia System by now. Even though these were giant stars their light did not go on forever. Xander was fairly certain that they had not entered any pathways yet. They had not been prepped for travel through these. But surely they would be entering these in time. As it was the only known way to travel extremely long distances. And the Gadoran's home system was a very long way from here, according to Hadik.

His mind went back to Riad. And Jelina. And Arielle. And Mondeus. He felt a sudden tightening in his chest. Were they looking for him? Did they think he was dead? How was Arielle doing? He had no way of knowing. He had to do something now. If the Gadorans entered the pathways, it would be too late.

He saw out of the corner of his eye that Hadik had returned to the main level. Hadik was with the comatose Gadoran. He appeared to be talking to him. Was he giving him some sort of treatment? Again, Xander's limited understanding of the Gadorans way of life made it impossible for him to tell.

Xander waved at Hadik, as he looked over towards him. After a few moments Hadik came over. He looked worried as he took a seat next to Xander.

"How is he doing?" Xander asked.

"My brother will not live much longer. I fear he will not survive this journey," Hadik said.

With an appropriate amount of empathy in his voice Xander responded "I am sorry to hear that."

"There are some good doctors in Aqualon. The large moon where we came from. They would be able to help him," he continued.

Hadik shook his head.

"Bodak commanded that we do not stop until we get back to our home world. Regardless of the circumstances," Hadik said sadly.

"Is he...is he your real brother?" Xander asked haltingly. He was not sure as Hadik had referred to the other Gadorans as brothers. Maybe the clarity was lost in the translation.

"He is the youngest of my three brothers. It was his first trip on a cargo ship to a distant planet," Hadik said slowly.

"He left two young daughters at home. Every time he was awake, he spoke about them," Hadik said sadly.

Xander felt the emotion from Hadik. This was an opportunity. An opportunity to share and be understood. He decided to wait no more.

"Do you have a few minutes?" he asked Hadik.

Hadik nodded.

"Can we talk some more?" Xander asked.

The older man nodded again.

For the next half of an hour so, Hadik listened. And listened well. Mostly nodding his head at times. To show that he understood. He spoke little. An occasional word of surprise. Or to have something clarified.

Xander started at the beginning. And told Hadik about his mother. Who was lost in an expedition, when he was very young. And to this day, his father and himself and Jelina still held out hope. Told him about their trip outside their home system. Their vacation and Aqualon. Hadik was a bit surprised that they were visitors to this system too. He had thought they were from the neighboring planets. Told him about their planned trip to Riad. And the ill fated camping trip. Later returning to find their spaceship missing.

Hadik bowed his head for a moment. Xander could not read his expression. He was not sure if it was that of guilt or shame. But something along those lines. Nonetheless, he motioned to Xander to continue. Xander proceeded to tell Hadik about Jelina. And Mondeus. And Arielle. Her injury. Followed by her severe illness. And in what critical condition she was in when Xander last saw her. That he did not know if she was still alive. And how desperately she needed medical attention if she were to survive.

Hadik understood only too well. His brother was in the same condition at this very moment. He was surprised that no adults were with them. In fact, the Gadorans were not sure exactly who made up the crew of the Pelican 25. They never imagined it would be all teenagers. And they did not understand the lack of range of the communication devices that Xander and company possessed. That the ship was actually needed to get longer range communication. The Gadoran's technology far exceeded this. They took for granted that any visitors would possess communication devices that would be able to contact the neighboring moons.

They were delighted to awake and find the ship unoccupied. Almost at their doorstep. They thought that luck was *finally* on their side. They had wanted to leave immediately. But were disappointed that the newly found ship did not have the capabilities to travel to their distant system. That is why they had to hide it. And make the necessary modifications. Fortunately, they had kept all the undamaged components of their own ship.

They were aware that at least some of the occupants of the Pelican 25 had returned to the area. But they had decided to keep a low profile to avoid potential conflict. Bodak had directed them to use force if necessary. They hoped that they would not have to. Little did Hadik realize, until now, that he and the other Gadorans may have just imposed their own terrible fate on someone else.

And then Xander made his request. One that surprised even Hadik.

Would Hadik help him persuade the others to turn the Pelican 25 around and head back to Aqualon? There his brother could get medical treatment. And live. And Xander would be able to get help. To return to Riad and rescue Jelina and Mondeus. And Arielle, if it were not too late already.

Hadik looked at Xander for a long time. Finally he said,

"If this were entirely up to me, I would consider it." Hadik paused for a moment.

"I know Bodak very well. He would not do it," he added.

"You can get help on Aqualon. They will find commuter ships to take you back to your home systems. You will have to be relayed but they will get you there eventually," Xander pleaded.

"Bodak does not trust strangers," Hadik said.

"As I told you before, I have known him for a long time. He would be very concerned about being punished by the authorities there if he returns. Under Gadoran law stealing a ship is a very serious offence. It is punishable by death in some cases. Let alone kidnapping someone. So I am very sure, he will not agree," Hadik explained.

"After so long, he and many of the Gadorans, see this as our only opportunity to return home. To our previous lives and the families that we left behind, so long ago. And nothing would stop them now."

"I also think that, if my brother was not so ill, I might not have considered it," Hadik said truthfully.

"In a few hours, it will not matter anyway," Hadik continued.

Xander guessed it before Hadik even said it.

"We would be entering the space conduits or what you call the Pathways," Hadik said.

IX.

It had seemed as if they would have never made it. The last several hundred meters appeared to be an eternity. An eternity within a trip that itself was an eternity. They had stopped too many times to count. They had stiff arms and wooden legs. Both Jelina and Mondeus were afraid that they might drop Arielle. Forty more steps they had counted. And then that was too much. Thirty more, take thirty more steps. And they got closer. And then it was only twenty at a time before they rested her down. And then ten steps as they were stumbling, almost falling over with each step. Ten more steps. They were crouching lower to the ground, pulled down by the weight they were carrying. Weight that felt at least twenty times heavier than when they started.

All the while Arielle's eyes were closed. They hoped that she was still in a coma and thus not able to feel any discomfort. And that she would survive this trip. When they first began to stop to rest, they would look at her chest, to make sure that she was still breathing. Then as they went beyond exhaustion, they hardly saw anything. There was just a single minded thought in their heads. Get to the cave. Get to the cave at all costs with Arielle. Nothing else mattered. They finally did. They would never be able to fully describe that trip to anyone. Words could not describe the experience.

But now they were sitting in the Gadoran's large dwelling. Still stiff and tired.

But in light and warmth. As much as they wanted. In a more comfortable environment than they had been for a long time. Having drank as much water as possible. The systems in the cavern were still intact. Mondeus adjusted the heat. Even in the days, when it was hot outside, the underground dwelling remained cool.

They had placed Arielle on a bed in one of the rooms in this cavern. She was breathing regularly. They spoke to her and she opened her eyes briefly. They were delighted. A few minutes after they laid her down, some sound escaped her lips. Unintelligible but it was enough for them. It fuelled Mondeus and Jelina.

Jelina looked around. They were starting to get hungry. She found food. She did not know the exact nature of it. Looked like dried vegetables and preserved meat. *Perhaps the Aliens were here long enough to extract these from the environment*, she thought. They were in an area where there were plates and a table. She figured this served as a kitchen and dining area. Electrical heating was not a problem. So she set about trying to make a meal for them. Either soup or broth could describe her attempts.

Mondeus was not even sure where the power came from. But it was central as everything he turned on worked. He was certain that the Aliens had advanced technology to generate and store power in ways that he did not quite understand. *This is great,* Mondeus thought. An idea flashed through his mind. Perhaps he could use some of this power to send signals for help. It was fleeting. He realized if this was the case, the Aliens would not have been shipwrecked here for such a long period of time.

As he got warmer he became hungrier. He was thinking much more clearly too. Jelina brought over some of the food to him. He had never tasted anything as good. Finished it in a hurry. And got some more. Jelina went over to Arielle. She sat gently by her bedside. And was determined to try to feed her. Mondeus brought a chair over and sat too. He insisted that Jelina have some soup first. She reluctantly complied. And very quickly, returned her attention to Arielle. At first, Arielle would not open her mouth. But ever so slowly she accepted small sips of thin soup. Little by little. With her eyes half closed. Like an infant. Jelina was patient. And lovingly caring. More than any trained nurse could hope to be. Her maternal instinct was very much evident.

After Jelina was finished, she and Mondeus just sat there. In silence but preoccupied. With dozens of thoughts churning through their heads. Mainly about their current predicament. Some time passed and then they both noticed it. Arielle opened her eyes. Fully open this time. And tried to speak. *Words!*

"Wh...?"

"Where?" they heard her say.

They wondered if she was going to ask for Xander. As that was at the forefront of their minds.

"Where, where are we?" she finally uttered.

Mondeus and Jelina were overjoyed. Not only did she speak. She was coherent! And aware of her surroundings; that they were different from before. Maybe it was the warm soup. Maybe she was turning the corner. They fervently hoped so regardless of the reason. As they tried to offer her an optimistic response, she closed her eyes again. Her regular breathing told them that she had gone back to sleep.

Mondeus was getting sleepy too. He had been through some exhausting times. Despite this, he wanted to look around the Gadoran abode before he fell asleep. He had learnt too much from Xander. Too much for his age. He shared his plans with Jelina. She did not object. But for now, she preferred to stay with Arielle. He would be within earshot and she knew that they needed to gather as much information as possible. It could only help them in the near future.

They had decided they were all going to sleep close to Arielle tonight. Their surroundings were much more comfortable than previous nights. And they were warm and not hungry anymore. Arielle had shown glimpses of improvement. Or was it just the fact that her body was now warmer? Was it just transient? *And Xander? What about him? What had the Aliens done to him?* they thought. Try as they might, they could not shed these thoughts.

Mondeus shook his head to clear his thoughts as well as the heaviness of his eyelids. He decided to look a bit more closely at the farthest rooms of the cavern. Those were the ones that they had rushed through the last time they were here. Just before the tremors began. Even though he had been there before, everything looked different. He was surprised at how much he had missed the first time. Perhaps he was looking at it with different eyes. He now remembered how scared they were. Without even acknowledging it, both he and Jelina had been looking for a body then. A wounded or dead Xander was what their eyes had scanned for. Which they never found. Everything else was inconsequential at the time.

He remembered that the cave had a rear opening. He had inferred that from the light they saw coming through. Now that he was a bit more familiar with the lighting systems of the Gadoran, he flooded the entire distal area of the cavern with lights. It was not as large as the front main area. But not much smaller either. There seemed be even more compartments than the front living area. It was also clear that a lot of this area was used as storage space. A wide variety of things filled the rooms. From what looked like abandoned computers to instruments and gadgets that Mondeus had no familiarity with. He also found basic tools like those used for farming. As well as scrap metal and what seemed to be pieces of the damaged spaceship.

Mondeus moved quickly from room to room, taking in as much as he could. He made a mental note of what could be of value to them. And what he might need to return for. He was sure he would be back in these storage rooms.

It was then that he found him. In one of the storage rooms at the rear of the cave. Along with a few other items from the Pelican 25. Just laying there immobile. His beloved Tytum!

"Jelina, Jelina," he called.

His voice carried eerily through the connecting area to the front of the cave.

Jelina heard him. And recognized the excitement of in Mondeus's voice. Not one of distress. Clearly a positive tone. She came running up to the area. They were not sure how they missed him the night before. But there was Tytum. Lying, sprawled on his side. Next to other discarded items. His power almost down to nothing.

"I found him," Mondeus cried as Jelina came bursting through the door.

"I see," Jelina smiled.

It was the first smile from her for days. Finally some joy! In the artificial light, with strands of her hair sticking out, she looked pretty. She was very happy for Mondeus. He had found what was for him, the equivalent of a family member.

"He will need some work but I think I can get him back to normal," Mondeus continued with unbridled enthusiasm. His delight and happiness were contagious.

Jelina nodded. "He looks in great condition."

There was no way she was going to refer to Tytum as an "It" tonight.

X.

Xander knew he must act. And act soon. Or it would be too late and all would be lost. Some ideas had formed in his head. One in particular. He had to give it a try. It was a long shot but he knew he had to try.

It was almost impossible to get to the controls of the main level. This area had the most activity. The last time he moved close to it, Bodak did not hesitate to threaten him with force. Which, no doubt he would use again, if he needed to. But Xander had gained the trust of Hadik. Hadik was very likeable and this had not proved to be difficult. They shared a lot. And his closeness was rewarded with Hadik's trust. They had removed the magnetic locks from his arms. He was now able to move around freely, if allowed to. Xander noted with interest that only one Gadoran used his upper level room as quarters. The room he and Mondeus used as a bedroom. Xander also knew that there were some secondary controls for the ship there. He was not sure if the Gadorans had disabled them. Or modified them. They were connected to the main computers of the ship and were essentially placed there as a back up. One that circumvented the need to go to the main terminals in case of an emergency.

Xander had to operate on the assumption that those controls were still intact. He also had to have the right timing. He had to wait for the

Gadoran to leave that area. And hope that Hadik was still in the main cabin with him. Xander was sure that Hadik was the only Gadoran who would let him out of sight much less give him the liberty to move around the ship. The Gadoran, whose name Xander did not know, did leave Xander's sleeping quarters a couple of hours ago. He had gone to the lower level. Perhaps to see Bodak, and get his orders. Anyway, he had returned after just a few minutes. *That may not be enough time for me to do much,* Xander thought. Yet, he knew he had to try.

Hadik was deep in thought. He did not say much but stayed in the main cabin area. Xander figured out that it was probably not Hadik's turn to be on duty. But he didn't mind staying close to his brother. As a result, Xander saw a lot of him. This allowed the other Gadorans to leave Xander alone and lessened the necessity of keeping a close eye on him. An announcement came over the general address system of the ship. It was Bodak's voice. Hadik translated it for Xander. They were to prepare for pathway travel in two hours. Clearly they were at the periphery of the Ixodia system now. And were preparing to head to another system. There was no way for Xander to know the length of these Pathways. The point of no return for Xander loomed ahead. It was very alarming, to say the least.

Xander then noticed that the Gadoran from the upper level came to the main level and then disappeared. He was not sure if Hadik noticed that actual event as from time to time, the other Gadorans did move around the main level. Xander decided to make his move. He told Hadik that he had left something in his old bedroom. And wanted to get it to show it to Hadik. Hadik nodded nonchalantly. *That was easier than I expected,* Xander thought, as he headed up the very familiar stairs. With his palms cold and sweaty and his heart pounding in his chest, he tried to think coherently.

* * * * *

Mondeus and Jelina quickly headed back to Arielle's room. They did not want to leave her alone for any length of time. Not again. They had imagined how frightened she must have been when they had gone searching for Xander. And when she found out she was all alone as the tremors came. They still could not imagine how she managed to drag herself out of that cave. Without any help. It was a minor miracle. When they had left her she was barely conscious. But they were incredibly thankful she was able to move. Because there was no longer a cave where they had left her!

With Tytum in tow, Mondeus lagged behind Jelina. Mondeus decided to carry him to speed things up. It was a lightweight robot after all. Made of an ultra light titanium alloy. Mondeus was happy that the Gadorans did no damage to him. They probably had no use for him. At the time anyway. But they must have recognized his potential usefulness. Otherwise they would not have thrown him in storage.

Mondeus was also willing to bet that they knew little of the program that Tytum carried. The one that had tried to communicate and locate him. Mondeus had designed it himself. And as far as he knew, it was unique to Tytum. That surely would have been a reason to destroy him. It was a pity that Tytum's communication was only short range. It was never built for anything more than that. And Mondeus would bet a years allowance that his signal was only strong enough to reach them when the Gadorans had opened the huge doors of the cavern. As time passed, his power would have faded and thus his signal had become weaker.

He left the rest of the exploration for the next day. They needed to get some rest. And some good sleep. Mondeus decided to use the overnight hours to power up Tytum. They would have some company tomorrow.

Tytum would be able to communicate and perform little chores by then. He might prove useful yet again. This inanimate friend of Mondeus. Actually, friend of them all.

XI.

As Xander entered his own room, he saw that not much had been altered. A big contrast to the main level. A deep breath escaped him as he noted that the secondary terminals were still in place. Without a moment's hesitation he headed for the far corner and sat down at the computer controls. As he stared at the screens, his heart fell. The computers were running a program that was entirely unfamiliar to him. He could not even understand the script, let alone the data. The Gadorans had pretty much reprogrammed the Pelican 25 systems! Configured it to travel to their distant world. Most likely by adding the systems from their own spaceships. Programs that they had kept all these years.

Xander sat at the terminal for what seemed to be a long time. It was less than a minute. There must be a way. Xander's current fields of study at the Plato schools included Astronomy, Robotics and Computer Sciences. He wracked his brain to find something useful. He knew that if he could log in, with some luck he could alter the commands of the ship. It all came down to whether the Gadorans had *erased* the old programs of the Pelican 25. There was a chance that these still existed. Xander thought it all depended on how large the programs of the Gadoran's old ship were. If they had merely bridged their systems to that of the Pelican 25, then the original programs of the Pelican 25 existed. If they were short on space, they could have erased those. For once, he thought that time was in his favor. The Gadorans had had to modify so much in such a short time, that they would not have done anything that was not absolutely necessary.

Xander knew that he had to try and hack into these computers. There was no other way. It was risky but everything was relative now. Options were severely limited. He manually turned off an adjunctive system at one of the secondary terminals. And then restarted it. He prayed that no major current ship operations hinged on this. And it would go unnoticed. As he was restarting this sequentially, he made his move. Using the manual controls, he tried hacking into the system. After a few anxious moments and with the help of some rogue techniques he had learnt in school, he was in. No doubt helped by the games he played with Mondeus. Most of the time they were to keep Mondeus's company. And he would have never guessed that, one day, they would potentially save his life.

One he was in, he knew the Pelican 25 systems as well as anyone. This time an audible gasp escaped from his lips. The original programs of the Pelican 25 were still intact! He headed straight for the emergency section. He had already planned what he had to do. At the moment, this first step was just as critical as anything else. He had to override the audible alarms immediately. This he did quickly leaving the long range distress signals on. And as he was getting to the most important part of what he set out to do, he heard footsteps outside his door. He froze. So close and yet so far. He held his breath waiting for the Gadoran to enter the room. And alert the others.

It never happened. The footsteps faded. As they went down the short hallway to Jelina and Arielle's room. One of the other Gadorans must have been using that room as quarters too. Xander had not noticed. Perhaps that Gadoran was also asleep for an extended period time. Or may have come and gone when Xander was asleep. In any event, Xander had to be quick. And quiet.

His fingers found life again. He accessed the protocol he wanted to. The emergency unmanned protocol. Existing solely in the event that they were all incapacitated and unable to fly the ship. It would override all other commands. It was a core system. It was relatively easy. Xander quickly found their coordinates for their penultimate destination. It was stored in the Pelican 25 under their destinations. That of Aqualon. He entered his code. Only two of these existed. One for him. And one that was used by the co-pilots. The one which Mondeus and Jelina had. And they could not be altered by any other data input. It was secure personal identification codes that existed only in their memories. Validation was done instantaneously by his retinal scan which was taken as he was sitting at the terminal. Without a moment's hesitation, he did it. Activated the emergency unmanned protocol.

It was irreversible now. The Pelican 25 would return to Aqualon. On its own. The only person who could abort its course would be Xander, Jelina and Mondeus. Xander was the only one on board. And he would have to enter his code. No doubt he was now in dangerous territory. The Gadorans would figure out sooner or later that he had something to do with the ship changing course. And Bodak would probably try to force him to do something about it. He must prepare himself for that likelihood.

Xander tiptoed down the stairs to the main cabin. His heart was pounding like a sledgehammer in his chest. No one seemed to have noticed him. Hadik was sitting beside his sick brother. He was not sure if Hadik saw him return as he headed back to the lounge area in a corner of the main cabin. Where the language machine was located. And where he had had many conversations with Hadik. He tried to calm himself without much success. A couple of the Gadorans passed through the cabin as he sat there. On their way to the lower level and attending to tasks unknown to him. They looked quite busy and occupied. Perhaps relating to preparation for Pathway travel.

Xander knew them all by appearance now. There was Bodak and Gadin. Hadik and his ill brother. And four Gadorans whose names he was not too sure of. They called out to each other and he had surmised that Radan and Mordak were the names of two of them. Radan was an older one who had stopped by to speak with Hadik in Xander's presence. Mordak was a younger one whom Bodak seem to interact with the most. It was Mordak who first sounded the alarm.

He had just taken a look at the controls of the main cabin and shrieked. He let out an excited yell. Bodak came running up and soon all the Gadorans followed. There was a lot of excitable chattering and then some shouting from Bodak as he pointed to the controls. Xander did not understand a word of what was said. But he knew what was happening. Mordak was the first to discover that the ship had changed course. He alerted the other Gadorans. None of them seem to know why. Two of the Gadorans sat at the controls and Xander noticed that they were frantically trying to input data and alter the course. Xander noticed that they were shaking their heads in dismay. Most likely because everything that they were doing was being rejected. And the more they tried without success, the louder Bodak became. Now shouting commands at the top of his voice. All in vain.

Xander had no idea what the Gadorans thought was wrong. One possibility was that the Pelican 25 was now unresponsive to the added controls of the Gadoran ship. That somehow there was a break in the bridge between the systems. Except that all the other systems seemed to be working quite fine. Mordak and Gadin continued at the controls, working as deftly as possible. Bodak was incessantly screaming instructions over their shoulders. Just about then Bodak pushed Gadin out of his seat and started trying himself. And he became angrier by the minute. The more he tried, the angrier he became. Time and again, he pointed at the instruments. Clearly the Gadorans knew they were off course and going in the wrong direction. Heading back to the inner Ixodia system.

Xander was thinking clearer now. He decided that to remain quiet, would be to rouse suspicion. He walked over to the area of commotion. With hand signals, he asked Hadik what was going on. Hadik looked at him strangely and turned away. Without any form of answer. It was only a couple of minutes that elapsed before Bodak saw him standing a few feet away to his right side. Xander noticed a change in Bodak's expression as Bodak looked directly at him. He felt transparent as if Bodak could tell exactly what he did. Bodak said something quite sharp. Xander did not understand any of it. All the Gadorans were quiet for the moment. Then Hadik spoke up. Bodak yelled at him. And then he turned to Mordak and shouted something to him.

Mordak disappeared and reappeared a few moments later. As Mordak was placing the magnetic handcuffs back on Xander, Xander realized what Bodak must have been saying. Hadik looked down at the floor as Xander was led away by Mordak. Mordak pushed him roughly into a chair in the corner of the cabin as the Gadorans kept working on the controls of the Pelican 25. Trying to alter the Pelican 25's now automated course. Something told Xander that his current situation was not too bad. But there was worse to come.

XII.

Jelina awoke first. She sat up suddenly. More with a feeling of panic than being rested. She had planned to wake up during the night and check on Arielle. Mondeus was still sleeping. Jelina quickly got up and turned up the lights in this little room that they occupied. Out of many, they had chosen to place Arielle in this one. For no good reason at the time, but it became their temporary headquarters.

She did not know how long they had slept. They were exhausted. It could have been a long time. And her body must have crashed in order to recuperate. Yet, she felt guilty as she quickly moved over to Arielle. To her surprise, Arielle was awake. Eyes wide open and appeared alert. Jelina had noticed some signs of improvement the previous evening, but this was pronounced. And unequivocal. It must have to do with the warmth, rest and food.

"Arielle," she whispered tentatively.

The beginnings of a smile showed on Arielle face. Still very worn and tired looking, but nonetheless, markedly improved compared to the previous couple of days.

"Where is Xander?" Arielle asked in a reasonably clear voice.

Jelina hesitated. Just enough for Arielle to know that she was withholding something. Jelina did not think that Arielle was ready for all the details yet. *In time,* she rationalized.

"He went to get help," Jelina offered.

Arielle did not pursue it.

"Where are we now?" Arielle asked.

Jelina was pleased that Arielle really did know that this was not the cave they had initially taken refuge in.

"We moved to a larger cave," Jelina explained.

"People lived here?" Arielle half asked, half stated.

"Yes, it was inhabited at some time," Jelina explained. The evidence was all around them. There was no denying this. She did not have to say how long ago it was that the cavern had occupants. Nor did she have to say who those occupants were.

The voices caused Mondeus to stir. As he heard Arielle speaking, he jumped up and ran over. And hugged her tightly, holding on to her.

"Arielle," he said almost breathless with excitement.

"Mondy," Arielle replied.

"I am so glad you are better," Mondeus said half to himself.

"Me too," Arielle said softly.

Jelina moved around to the other side of the bed and gave a big hug to Arielle as well. She did not understand why she didn't do it before. Too much had happened that Arielle did not know about. And it had weighed heavily on her mind. The hug that Mondeus gave Arielle said it all. Relief, joy and optimism all mixed into one. She was better now. And they were now counting their blessings one at a time. For now, they were glad that Arielle was with them again.

They were silent for a while. Jelina still knew that they had to get help soon. It seemed as if Arielle's body was clearing the infection and it toxins from her bloodstream. Her immune system was finally winning. But her leg was still very much red and swollen. And she could still possibly lose it. At the very minimum, she still had a fracture that needed a medical specialist, to prevent deformity of her leg.

Mondeus noticed that light was coming from the distal part of the cave. He had turned off the artificial lighting in the storage area of the cavern. Just in case they would need that power later on. It was sunlight. Streaming through an opening at the back of the cave. He had not noticed that additional doorway last night. More than likely due to the darkness outside, he thought. Jelina was again trying to get some warm broth for Arielle to drink. Arielle still looked tired. The conversation had taken some effort out of her. Mondeus decided he would take a look.

It was later in the day than he had expected. Already mid morning with both suns high in the sky. They had slept for at least ten hours. As

Mondeus walked out of the rear entrance of the huge cave, he was surprised yet again. The Gadorans had chosen well. Or they had designed everything to meet their needs. *They must have been here for quite some time,* thought Mondeus.

The rear entrance of the cave led out into a small valley. It was almost completely surrounded by the low hills. One could not really stumble upon it from outside as it was protected by the hills which dropped off suddenly into this small valley. Even the light that came though the rear entrance of the cave, would not be there all day, as the suns needed to be at a particular angle for that to happen.

And the clearing itself. It was a well-tilled garden! With numerous shoots and vegetable-like plants. As well as plants with pods and seeds. Mondeus figured that these were edible beans and grains that the Aliens had cultivated. As he surveyed what was in front of him, he noted there was also a small stream at the bottom of the valley, that disappeared under one of the large rocky hills. Whomever had chosen this site clearly had done so with a lot of planning. And had planned for the long term. This was no overnight venture.

Mondeus was mulling over his new discovery, when it dawned upon him that the rear entrance of the cave was most likely created. To lead specifically to this clearing. In fact, he was almost certain it was. As many of the rooms in the cavern were. It seemed as if the Aliens had technology to assist them. And they did not seem short of a power source either. Another thing Mondeus now knew, him and the girls would have no shortage of plant food. Not in the short term anyway.

As he gathered some beans and vegetables to take to Jelina, his mind was still racing. Things were looking up at the moment but their overall situation was still bleak. Time was still of the essence. Arielle had temporarily improved yet she needed urgent medical attention for her leg.

He was almost afraid to think of Xander's fate. If they could get out of here, maybe they could get help to him. That is, if it were not already too late.

He was initially hopeful that he could find a way to establish some kind of long range communication. With all the power and computers sitting around the cave, it seemed possible. Somewhere in the recesses of his mind, a little voice told him that it was very unlikely. If it could have been done, the people living here would not have been here for so long. Yet, he felt he was obligated to try. Perhaps they might get lucky and make contact with someone else who was visiting Riad and happen to be within range.

He knew deep down that help would come soon. How soon he had no way of knowing. They must be recorded as missing by now. The authorities would have to do something. He just hoped it would be the earlier part of "soon." In time for Arielle. He was hoping that they would send a search party to look for them. Suddenly, another distressing thought crossed his mind. What if a search party came to Riad and could not find them? He had no way of communicating with them. The search party would have no way of determining their exact location. It was indeed possible that they could come and leave Riad without finding them.

With some effort Mondeus pushed that thought out of his mind. He tried to return to the present. He just hoped that they would not have to use this kitchen garden for too long. And that Arielle would not have a relapse. *And what about Xander?* he thought. For some strange reason, his mind would not allow him to pursue that line of thought.

* * * * *

It must have been close to two hours now. The commotion on the deck of the Pelican 25 continued unabated. All the Gadorans, barring Hadik's ill brother, were there. And they were chattering all the time. Xander did not understand much barring occasional words that would seem to translate as agreement or disagreement. He was within earshot and could see what they were doing for the most part. Bodak kept giving the commands and from their body expressions, they did not seem to be making progress. Finally Bodak turned around and yelled something to Mordak. Mordak got up and headed straight for Xander. Even though Xander was expecting this, he still felt a dread overcoming him.

Mordak pulled him roughly to his feet. Xander almost fell over as he tried to stand. He had no balance as his hands were magnetically locked together.

Mordak pretty much dragged him over to the center of the main cabin, next to the main controls. Despite the fact that Xander was slightly taller than Mordak, the Gadorans were stoutly built. Xander knew he had no chance of overpowering any one of them. He tried to think and plan for what was ahead.

Bodak did not waste any time. He did not even bother with the translation machine. He pulled his weapon and pointed it to the side of Xander's head. He motioned to the controls of the Pelican 25 with a sideways nod of the head. Without using any words, his question was quite clear. Bodak looked directly into his eyes. All the other Gadorans held their breath. Xander knew if he ever had to take a stand, it was now or never. He looked straight back at Bodak and slowly shook his head. He did not avert his gaze even though this took tremendous effort on his part. Xander made his intention clear. He did not know what the problem was. Bodak yelled at him this time. Hadik stepped forward and feebly protested. Bodak waved his weapon at Hadik, and snarled something.

Xander did not understand any of what was said. With a subdued look, Hadik stepped away. The moment was tense. All the other Gadorans remained silent. All one could hear was the engines of the Pelican 25.

Hadik returned moments later with the translating machine. He placed it next to Xander.

"Bodak wants to know if you changed the ship's course?" Hadik asked slowly. Xander noticed that Hadik was avoiding looking at him.

"No," Xander replied, sounding more confident than he was feeling.

"Bodak wants to know if you can fix it," he continued.

Xander was about to say no, when he realized that may not be the wisest choice. After all, he was supposed to know these systems inside out. It was their ship.

"I can try," Xander said hesitantly.

Xander sat at one of the main controls and motioned to Mordak, who uncuffed him. He started working at one of the terminals. Slowly at first. Then more quickly. He knew regardless of the data showing on the screen, if he did not enter his personal identification codes, the ship would not override the emergency protocol. He deliberately accessed some of the residual systems of the Pelican 25. He gave the impression that he was working on changing the ship's course. He knew that the Gadorans would not be able to understand the script nor follow the commands he inputted. Many minutes passed with the Gadorans anxiously looking over his shoulder. Nothing happened.

Slowly and purposefully, Xander shook his head, as if in frustration. Bodak was becoming agitated again. Xander continued to work. Most of the work was accessing systems and displaying data. Whilst at the terminals, he managed to gleam that they were heading to Aqualon at a very high speed. Using the pull of that binary star, their return trip would be much quicker than the outgoing trip. This pleased him but he was careful not to show it. He still had no idea what the Gadorans would do to him as they approached Aqualon.

He continued to shake his head to show no success. Bodak shouted something into the translating machine. Again, Xander did not understand what he was saying. Hadik repeated it more slowly.

"What is the problem?" Hadik asked.

"The ship controls would not accept any of my commands," Xander said truthfully.

Bodak shouted at him again. This time Hadik did not translate.

"It would not accept any of the data that I am inputting," Xander continued, a bit more meekly.

Another bout of shouting by Bodak and Mordak quickly stepped into action.

He and another Gadoran grabbed Xander roughly. And dragged him up the short flight of stairs. Into the little compartment, at the rear of his own quarters. Where he first woke up on the ship after they left Riad. They did not forget to replace his magnetic handcuffs this time. Xander was thus returned to his private prison cell. Now, he would have no idea of what the Gadorans were doing. And if they were to somehow succeed in getting back the Pelican 25 on their course, he would not be able to tell. Xander knew that they did possess technology and systems that he did not understand. Most of it taken from their old ship. Thus he must consider the possibility of the Gadorans eventually succeeding in overriding his core commands. One thing he knew for sure, they were an extremely determined bunch. And they would not stop trying.

PART 6
Balkan

I.

The room was very large. Five people were seated at a huge table in the middle of it. The Chief of Security of Aqualon was doing most of the talking. Chief Papuan was a large man and when he spoke, people usually listened. On his right side sat the Deputy of Security of Aqualon. Deputy Magellin had briefed the chief on all the known facts concerning the missing Pelican 25. On his left side sat two of their assistants.

Seated across from them was a man who was in his mid-to-late forties. Normally cheerful, he looked distinctly worried now. His eyes, which were usually twinkling, darted from person to person. His voice showed a calmness that he did not feel. Balkan Ulysses Villanova was extremely worried. Both of his children and their two friends had been reported missing for more than a week now. He was first contacted after they had failed to file their second consecutive travel report to Central station. He knew that these were automated reports by the ships computers so he decided not to worry too much. But when the third report was not received, he knew something had gone wrong. He had made immediate plans to travel to Aqualon as the authorities there had made little to no progress in finding the Pelican 25.

Chief Papuan was very civil and understanding. And Dr. Villanova knew that getting adversarial with him would only hinder their progress. Essentially, they needed to get a large search party on the ground on Riad. To date, all their communication and scanning systems had failed to locate the Pelican 25. Of course, their scanning was focused on Riad, which the Pelican 25 had left days ago. Fortunately, the orbit of Riad was getting closer to Aqualon again. And it would take only a relatively short trip to get there. Balkan Villanova wanted to go with the search party. The Chief needed some convincing. It was a matter for the authorities he insisted. It would be a break of protocol for a civilian to travel on such a search party. Dr. Villanova did not have the necessary training, he explained.

Balkan knew that this conversation was heading in the direction that would benefit him least. He decided to take a step back.

"Can we open some of the windows, please?" he asked.

Chief Papuan seemed surprised at this question, but there was no reason why he couldn't. At the very least, this could placate Dr. Villanova.

"Sure," he said, nodding to one his assistants.

The warm breeze came through the windows and filled the large room. It was coming directly from the ocean. It did have a positive effect on Balkan Villanova. He would keep the windows open all day, if he worked here. He did understand though, why it did not seem to make a difference to the rest of the people in the room. They were used to it.

Balkan Villanova grew up with many things but open windows and warm breezes were not among them. He was a Voyager. And for centuries now they lived on space stations. These had become very large in the last few generations. Essentially they were orbiting cities. With everything from large Universities, shopping malls and recreation fields. But no windows that could be opened. Nor warm breezes from Oceans. He spent a fair bit of time working on Mars and the moon. The Lunites were just as lacking as the Voyagers where this was concerned. Their cities were also in bubbles, with enhanced gravity. In recent years though, since his children had started attending school on Earth, he had gotten to experience this joy more frequently. Whenever he traveled to Earth, he almost always tried to stay close to the equator. There it was warm anytime of the year. He suspected, although he had no definitive evidence, that his ancestors were from the warmer latitudes of Earth.

He closed his eyes and cleared his brain.

"We need to have more than one plan," Balkan Villanova insisted.

"If the search party comes up empty, we would lose days," he continued.

"We would send a search and rescue party to Riad later today," Chief Papuan said.

"And what if they are not on Riad?" Balkan probed.

"Where else could they be?" the Chief asked rhetorically.

"Our scanners have not detected any spaceship accidents in the Ixodia system in the last couple of weeks. And the last recorded flight plans of the Pelican 25 were to Riad," he droned on.

Balkan knew all of this already. He just wanted to cover all the bases. Suppose they were not on Riad. And if not, by the time the Search and Rescue party returned, it would be several more days. Valuable days would be lost. This did not sit well with him and he did not want all his eggs to be in one basket. But Balkan was not thinking objectively and he knew it.

"Why can't we leave for Riad now?" he continued, with urgency in his voice.

The Chief smiled patronizingly. He knew that Dr. Villanova was extremely stressed. And he tried his best to be comforting.

"The orbits would be closest in a few hours," he said gently. "We would not get there any quicker by leaving now."

Balkan knew that the Chief was correct. He was silent for a few moments. He just did not know what to do for the next few hours as conflicting thoughts continue to race through his brain.

Chief Papuan looked around at his men. It seemed as if the meeting was over. Somehow he still felt inadequate.

"It should be a fairly straightforward mission," he offered, hoping to console Dr. Villanova.

"We have had to do this in the past," he said.

"Almost always, it is a communication problem. A couple of occasions, by the time we reached the moon in question, the kids had already left for Aqualon. Often times, they just lose of track of time and forget to check in," he explained.

Dr. Villanova nodded. He appreciated the effort the Chief was making.

Somehow though, he knew something had gone wrong. His kids were a very responsible lot. They would not just forget to check in for such a long time. And if an undamaged Pelican 25 was on the surface of Riad, the long range scanners would have most probably picked it up.

"Dr Villanova...," the Chief was beginning to say something, when he was interrupted by a short beep. All of the other security men including Deputy Magellin also had their paging devices activated. Some sort of emergency. Before he could look at the device, there was an urgent knock on the door and a uniformed officer walked in.

"I need to brief you sir," he said to the Chief as the other men looked on.

The Chief nodded to his deputy, indicating that he should handle it. The Officer stood his ground.

"This needs *your* immediate attention, sir," the Officer insisted.

"OK," the Chief said waiting for the Officer to continue.

"Privately sir," the Officer said respectfully.

II.

Jelina was still sitting at Arielle's bedside when Mondeus returned. They were exchanging occasional words in soft voices. Mondeus did not know how much Arielle remembered about their plight. She had slipped in and out of consciousness for a few days. He was sure Arielle knew they were in dire straits but he had no way of knowing how much of the details Arielle had absorbed or could remember.

He told Jelina about the garden and how well cultivated it was. In the presence of Arielle. She seemed to understand everything he said. Mondeus knew they would have to tell her about Xander soon. They could not keep it from her forever. She would ask again soon anyway. Maybe he would leave it up to Jelina. She could explain things much better than he did. Technically, they had not lied. Xander did go to get help. But he was not on this moon as Jelina and Mondeus implied.

Mondeus walked over to the adjacent room without saying anything to Jelina. She followed him after a few minutes. She sensed Mondeus wanted to tell her something. And not in the presence of Arielle.

"What is it Mondy?" she asked cautiously

Arielle could see them talking but could not hear them.

"Did you tell her?" Mondeus asked, referring to Xander. It was the elephant in the room that they were ignoring.

"Not yet," Jelina said slowly.

"I have been thinking," Mondeus continued.

She waited for him to elaborate.

"They would have recorded us as missing by now. And will send a search party for us."

"I am hoping so too," Jelina concurred.

"How soon I do not know," Mondeus said. Jelina noted that he was sounding very much like Xander. Much older than his age.

Jelina nodded.

"I don't know how efficient the authorities on Aqualon are," Mondeus continued. "But that is where the team will originate from, not from our System."

Jelina was still waiting for him to make his point.

"We must help them to find us," he said finally.

Jelina understood fully. The authorities would try to find them by finding the Pelican 25. And there was no Pelican 25 on Riad! Which meant they could not really pinpoint their exact location. Their exact landing site would have been stored on the Pelican 25 database. And that could not be accessed currently. At this time Mondeus and Jelina were doubtful that the Pelican 25 was even in the Ixodia system. Without help a search for them could be tedious and time consuming. And time was of utmost importance. Especially for Arielle and Xander.

"How can we help them?" Jelina prodded.

"Two possible ways," Mondeus said.

Jelina could guess the first one but had no clue of the second one. Still she wanted Mondeus to say it.

"With some time, I could power up the two remaining communication devices," he said slowly. "That would allow us to get a range of a couple of hundred miles."

Jelina had an immediate concern but kept it to herself for the moment. *Did this mean one of us would have to stay outside all the time?* After all, there was limited range deep within the cave.

Instead, she asked "How long would it take?"

"I am not sure," Mondeus said truthfully. "The Aliens seemed to have a lot of power here, but I am not familiar with their technology. I am sure I could tap into it with some digging around. But it will take time."

Jelina was confident that he could.

"And the other possibility?" she nudged.

"The other way is quite simple. But I do need your help."

"What is it?" she asked anxiously.

"We could mark out a large sign in the sand. In the clearing where we landed. It should be visible from above. With the letters H-E-L-P."

Jelina blinked. Simple but ingenious.

"How about the wind?" she asked.

"We would have to do it every morning," Mondeus said.

"We could do it with rocks but that would take a lot more time," Mondeus explained.

"What are we waiting for?" Jelina cried. "It is still not too late for today!"

"Let's go," Mondeus agreed, as they rushed off to tell Arielle first.

* * * * *

Xander must have dozed off. Sitting in the small compartment, with his hands cuffed in front of him. He would have thought that it was impossible to sleep in such a position. He had been awake for some time before falling asleep. The Gadorans had left the door of the room slightly ajar and he could still hear voices coming from the main level. Faint, but unintelligible. Even if they were louder, he would not have been able to understand what they were saying.

With the monotonous droning of the Pelican 25 in the background and nothing to do, it was not surprising he fell asleep. He was not sure how long he had slept or what roused him. Even more importantly, he had no way of knowing if they were still on course for Aqualon. If they were, they should be approaching the inner system by now. For the hundredth time or so, he tried to move his arms apart. At about 12 inches, the magnetic force became too strong and that was as far as he could go. He was completely helpless now but he took solace in the fact that he had done all he could do.

And then he realized what had roused him. The voices of the Gadorans coming through the door was much louder now. Although he did not understand the words, he sensed there a newer urgent tone to them. He even detected some panic and anxiety. This suggested to Xander that something new was happening. And it was not what the Gadorans wanted. He hoped that they had not tampered with the ship in such a way that it was no longer space-worthy.

And then he heard the emergency broadcast on the Pelican 25. It was not in Xander's home language. But that of the main regional language of the Ixodia system. Xander was not fluent but skillful in this tongue. It was related to the language of Old Portuguese of the Originals. The Gadorans had received a communication via this tongue. It was fed into the main system of the Pelican 25 and broadcasted throughout the ship. What Xander heard made him want to shout for joy!

"Please identify yourself. Please identify yourself, Pelican 25."

"This is the Space Patrol of Aqualon."

A thousand thoughts must have passed through Xander's head in the next few seconds. All at once and in no particular order.

They have been found! Or rather the Pelican 25 was found.

They were still in the Ixodia system. But just as important, the Gadorans could not understand a word of what was just said.

"If you do not identify yourself, we will attempt to board your vessel," the communication continued.

Xander realized that this would be difficult and time consuming without the cooperation of the Pelican 25 crew. It would be a relatively simple exercise if the rear hatch was opened and the air compression adjusted for the other ship to dock. He had no doubt that they would do it. They must have picked up the emergency signal that the Pelican 25 emanated. This would have started when Xander activated the emergency protocol. The Patrols would assume if they got no response that the crew was injured or worse. And was unable to respond to them. It was only a matter of time before they attempt to board the Pelican 25. And that could pose a huge risk to them as the Gadorans could potentially be hostile. He wished he had some way to communicate with them.

The thought had barely left his head when he heard footsteps coming up the short flight of stairs. A very tired Hadik and Mordak appeared. Mordak grabbed him and dragged him down the stairs. Hadik followed dutifully.

Xander took in the scene before him. On the main video screen was a large patrol ship. Xander thought that it must be pretty close as the Gadorans were looking at it via the telescopic systems. Bodak had the translator hooked up to the audio input. He was livid. Xander figured that Bodak was hoping the machine would translate for them. But the machine had not learnt yet. This was a completely different language from what Xander had used. And Xander knew he was of value again. They needed him to communicate with the Patrol ship.

Hadik asked him via the translator if he understood what the Patrol Ship was saying. Xander nodded. Hadik said something to Bodak.

Hadik asked Xander again "What did they say?"

"They are getting ready to board this ship if we do not answer," Xander translated. Bodak became even more furious, if that was at all possible. And again snapped something to Hadik, who dutifully relayed it to Xander.

"We will open up communication channels. We want you to talk to them," he said.

Xander agreed. He had no choice.

As the channels were opened, Bodak slowly said what he wanted to say. Directly into the machine. No need for Hadik this time.

"Pelican 25, do you copy?" the voice came from the Patrol ship again.

Xander said exactly what Bodak told him. As slowly as Bodak had said it.

"Do not attempt to board this ship. We have a prisoner."

The meaning was very clear. If they attempted to, harm would come to the prisoner.

But Xander added quickly before they could sign off, "Jelina is still on Riad."

There was a moment of silence before the Patrol ship responded.

"Copy. We will escort you back to Aqualon," the ship Patrol continued in a slow deliberate voice. Xander relayed this to the Gadorans.

With that Bodak snapped the channel shut and glared at Xander. Hadik averted his eyes. He knew Xander had added something to the message Bodak instructed him to deliver. He did not know what Xander had said as Xander had used the regional language of Ixodia. Xander looked down at the floor. The Gadorans made no effort to move him back to his confinement.

III.

Chief Papuan stepped into a private office adjacent to the large meeting room and closed the door.

"What is it?" he asked rather impatiently.

The Officer on duty looked directly at him and replied enthusiastically, "We just got word that the Pelican 25 was located."

"Great news," boomed the Chief. And before the Officer could continue, he asked "Why didn't you tell us all in the conference room?"

"It was not located on Riad Sir. It was found in the outer third of our System."

"What? They got lost in the Ixodia System?" the Chief asked incredulously.

"We doubt that. They were located by our Space Patrols in the Outer System," the Officer continued.

"An accident?" the Chief could not control his curiosity.

"Not likely" the Officer continued deliberately.

"It seems as if they were kidnapped and their ship hijacked."

"Kidnapped?"

"The Space Patrols told us that Xander Villanova is a prisoner in his own ship."

"They were ordered not to board. The kidnappers said if they tried to, they would harm the prisoner."

"However, the Patrols were confused by the fact that Xander said his sister is still on Riad."

"That does not make much sense," Chief Papuan said, still reeling from the news and conflicting bits of information he was receiving.

"Do you have the transcripts?"

The Chief was trying hard to find his feet. Crime in the Ixodia system, whilst not unheard of, was quite rare.

"Yes Sir," the Officer said.

The Chief led the way into the command center. The Officer replayed the recorded communication from the Space Patrols that had located the Pelican 25. Chief Papuan had him replay it several times. Eight times altogether.

Papuan was quite an astute man. He was often underestimated by his opponents. Perhaps his large size had something to do with it. Not always known for his politeness, he was often gruff and to the point with his subordinates. But he was in his true element now, gleaning as much information as possible from the recording.

Balkan Villanova and the rest of the security team were still in the large meeting room. Wondering what this new holdup was all about. Balkan was quite anxious for the mission to Riad to get underway. As soon as possible.

He did not think that Papuan was the type to stall. Yet he was getting more anxious with each passing minute.

Finally, Chief Papuan had something concrete to go on. He could formulate more precise plans. Papuan was one who believed in laying all the cards on the table. He had found over time that this was usually the best approach.

"Bring Dr. Villanova and Magellin in here," the Chief ordered.

As the Officer went to fetch them, Papuan listened to the recorded message one more time. He would brief the others later. For now, he must act.

"Dr. Villanova, we found the Pelican 25," he said bluntly.

Balkan Villanova eyes widened with excitement and relief at the same time. Before he could fully digest the news, the Chief continued,

"We think only your son is on board."

Balkan's relief turned to confusion. He looked from the face of Chief Papuan to the on duty Officer to the Deputy. The Deputy was just as confused and was waiting for Papuan to elaborate.

"Listen to this," the Chief said.

He played the recording for Balkan and his Deputy. Before they could even ask a question, the Chief Papuan spoke

"Is that your son's voice?" he asked.

"Yes, it is."

"Are you very sure?"

"I am 100 percent certain."

"Good," Chief Papuan said. He was all business now.

"It seems as whoever took your son prisoner took him alone. He clearly stated *"a"*prisoner, not prisoners. He also made a point to say that his sister was still on Riad. I deduce that he wants us to go rescue them and not focus solely on the Pelican 25."

"My guess is, his kidnappers did not speak our language and they forced him to talk to us. But he was smart enough to fit in the extra information we needed in his brief communication."

That did not surprise Xander's father. But his brain could not think clearly with all this new information. Multiple thoughts were racing through his head. Were the others unharmed on Riad? How would they have survived without the ship? What would happen to Xander on the Pelican 25?

The last question he addressed to Chief Papuan.

"Where is the Pelican 25 headed to?"

The answer to this one again brought surprise. And some relief.

"By present coordinates, it is headed directly back to Aqualon."

"What?" This did not make any sense.

"We think it is on autopilot by emergency protocol. It was picked up by our Patrols by its distress signal."

"What do we do now?" asked Balkan Villanova, who was rarely at loss for words or ideas.

"The Space Patrols have already asked for backup. I will order two more ships that are located in the region to escort the Pelican 25. The three Patrol ships will shepherd it back to Aqualon."

"OK," Balkan agreed. There was not much else he could say. His main concern though was not the Patrol Ships. It was his son's safety. And he knew that the Chief could not guarantee it.

"Our Search and Rescue team will leave for Riad within the hour. They were alerted earlier," the Chief said.

"Would you like to go with them?"

How quickly things changed, Balkan thought. Balkan realized that it would take more than a day before the Pelican 25 reached Aqualon. He would eat his nails all the way to his elbows by then.

"Thank you," he said quietly.

"Get ready then. The team will leave in forty five minutes sharp."

Gesturing to his Deputy, he added, "Magellin, you will lead that team. I want to be here when the Pelican 25 arrives."

IV.

Mondeus knew one thing for sure. The communication devices did not reach into the depths of the cave. There was a good chance that anyone trying to contact them would be unable to, if they stayed in the cave-dwelling. He had recharged the two units that they had remaining. From the clearing he could only reach Jelina if she was close to the mouth of the cave. And not at all if she was at the rear. Reception was sporadic where Arielle laid but nonetheless they left one of the devices with her. It would crackle on occasions but one could not decipher much of any message. This is probably what had happened with Tytum. He was not quite sure why the cave was so impermeable to signals. Other that being underground, it probably had to do with the properties of it rocky walls, he thought.

This posed a big problem for Mondeus and Jelina. After marking out their help sign in the clearing, they took turns at staying outside. They were hoping that someone would try to reach them. Actually Mondeus did most of the sentinel duties as Jelina took care of Arielle. Arielle had become very quiet again. They did not think that she was having a relapse but they could not be sure.

After a long discussion, they had decided to tell her about Xander. *Honesty is the best policy, isn't it?* Jelina thought. They told her how Xander and Mondeus had found the Pelican 25. And the Pelican 25 had left Riad with some strangers aboard. And Xander had gone with them. They had omitted some of the details but they did give her a fairly accurate picture of their current situation. It was a difficult and loaded conversation. Jelina did most of the talking, whilst Mondeus sat quietly nodding. Arielle was alert enough to know that Xander had not gone willingly with the strangers. And they all had no idea of where he was taken. And what had become of him. Or even if he was still in the Ixodia system. Arielle was awake but had hardly said a word since then. Now that she knew as much as they did, she had gone into her shell. Perhaps it was too much too soon.

Mondeus was torn between whether they should have told her or not. Jelina was the one who had convinced him to. If they had not told her today, they would have had to soon, Jelina rationalized. She was going to ask for details soon anyway. Of that they were sure. Mondeus did not tell her that he saw Xander being shot. Technically, he did not lie. He just omitted that information. That is how he consoled himself anyway. Jelina and Mondeus had reasoned that since they did not find Xander, he was alive. But they were not certain of that. Maybe, Arielle thought of it the other way. And that was more than enough reason for her to be ill again.

Mondeus and Jelina had had more time to assimilate all these events. And they were actively trying to get help. Not being immobile, it was impossible to comprehend Arielle's vantage point. And that may just have been the reason for their differing perspectives.

Mondeus tried to focus on the task at hand. How would they manage to communicate with anyone overnight? In the beginning he thought he would just have to stay outside. But he knew well from experience, this sandy moon trapped very little heat. And got quite cold overnight. That was not a good option at the present time. They had long lost their warming units. Buried under the rubble during the tremors.

He thought of staying close to the door of the cave. Sort of an in between area. Where he could get some heat and still have a chance of communicating with anyone looking for them. This was far from ideal. It would be a hit and miss situation. If someone was trying to scan for them using electromagnetic signals, they could miss them entirely. Worse yet, if a Search Party detected no one in this area they would move on to another area, he thought. They would probably not land unless they had the exact coordinates of their initial landing from the Pelican 25. He just hoped that they did the majority of the searching in the daylight hours.

And then a sudden insight jolted him. It was so simple that that he was surprised that he did not think about it before.

Tytum.

Of course, Tytum.

He rushed over to tell Jelina and Arielle about it.

"Tytum wouldn't freeze to death!" he exclaimed.

"What?" Jelina asked not following his school of thought.

Arielle was sitting up in bed and looked at him strangely. It was almost as if she was not there. She had really taken everything to heart now. And they did not know what to do about it.

"Tytum can withstand the cold," he continued.

Jelina still did not get it.

"We can leave him outside," Mondeus explained.

And then it dawned upon her.

"Of course, we can," she said upping the tone of her voice as she belatedly shared his excitement. Mondeus had powered up Tytum fully and it was as functional as ever.

"I can leave him outside the mouth of the cave, in the clearing overnight and I will stay inside. Not too far in but just where it is comfortable. Tytum would act as a relay for any signals. Coming in or going out!" he said triumphantly.

Jelina could not help but be optimistic too.

"Great idea," she said and came over and gave him a hug.

Perhaps it was just too much for Arielle, just lying there, to assimilate. All he got was a long questioning look. She seemed to understand but he could not tell whether she shared their optimism.

* * * * *

It seemed like it had been a very long time but Xander was certain it could not have been more than a couple of hours. The Gadorans had shut off the communicating channels with the Patrol Ship but kept the ship in sight on the video screen above the ship controls. Initially they were quite agitated and continued to work on trying to get the Pelican 25 to obey their commands. But ever so gradually their enthusiasm waned. They

216

continued working but it seemed as if their hope was fading. Bodak left for a few minutes and returned. Hadik went over and sat by the bedside of his ill brother. Xander never understood why the other Gadorans paid Hadik's brother so little mind. Perhaps they were accustomed to people hibernating for long periods of time.

As for Xander, no harm had come to him. In fact, no one paid him much mind. After the angry glares he had received and Bodak's episode of shouting at him, they all but ignored him. But that changed in a hurry when Mordak, who was sitting at the controls suddenly shrieked and pointed to the screen. They all looked up and jaws dropped open. Small at first, but getting larger with each passing moment, two more ships appeared on screen. As they continued to stare, the ships moved closer and essentially surrounded them.

Bodak finally decided to act. He opened the audio channels and demanded something. Of course, no one understood as he spoke in his native tongue. No response. He turned to Hadik, who had come over by now, and continued speaking. Again all Xander could do was to guess the meaning of what was said. Hadik spoke into the translator to Xander.

"Bodak wants you to talk to them."

"Ask them, what do they want?"

Xander complied and spoke to the Patrols.

"We want the safe return of Xander Villanova," the first Patrol ship replied, most likely the captain.

"We will not harm him, if you allow us to go free," Bodak relayed through Xander.

"Then you have to give us access to dock," the captain replied.

"No," Bodak indicated firmly.

"Currently you are on course to Aqualon, one of our larger inhabited moons in this system. We will escort you there and continue negotiations," the captain continued.

Xander said this slowly to Hadik so the exact meaning could be relayed to Bodak. He nodded. He understood.

"No harm will come to you, if you do not harm Xander Villanova. Understood?"

"Yes," Xander said after being given permission to say so.

"And if you do, we will have no choice but to take hostile actions," the Patrol ship captain continued. Xander was not sure that he wanted to translate this, but he did anyway.

Without saying a word, Bodak snapped shut the channel. He almost appeared to be resigned to his fate now. They were surrounded by three ships and he could not even command the Pelican 25, much less contemplate evasive action. Offensive action was also completely out of the question. They were now outnumbered three to one. But most importantly, the Pelican 25 ship was not designed for any kind of combat. The Patrol ships were.

The captain of the first Patrol ship let out a deep breath. It was a good conversation. They had been following the Pelican 25 for a couple of hours but they had no way of knowing what was happening on board. As he prepared to relay his update to Aqualon, he knew that Xander Villanova was alive and well for the moment. The hijackers of the Pelican 25 were unable to control the ship. And with the arrival of the extra Patrol ships, it was very unlikely that the mutineers would try anything rash.

V.

Mondeus awoke early. The suns were barely above the horizon but light came streaming through the opening of the cave. They had never fully replaced the large door. Before rousing Jelina, Mondeus checked his communicating devices. He had heard nothing overnight. But he checked just in case. No entry. He rushed out to see Tytum. Tytum was still active. Even though he was a robot, Mondeus did not like to leave him outside. But he had no choice. He quickly checked. Tytum had not picked up any new signals.

Mondeus hung his head in disappointment. He wasn't really expecting to be contacted overnight, yet he had been hopeful. He had tried to boost the range of their devices. He was not sure how successful he was. It had already been some time since they were stranded here. He had lost track of the exact number of days. Surely they would send a Search Party for them. The question was when. He didn't want to lose hope. If they had not found the Aliens' abode, they would have been starving by now. His thoughts turned to Xander. *How was he doing?*

He walked slowly back to Jelina. She opened her eyes. Arielle was sleeping. One look at Mondeus's face told her all she needed to know.

"No luck yet?" She attempted to be cheerful, with emphasis on the "yet." Mondeus shook his head.

Jelina got up.

"Let's go and put up the sign again," Jelina suggested as she continued to sound optimistic.

She whispered to Arielle that they were going outside for a short time. Arielle opened her eyes and acknowledged. And as they were about to leave, she said in a clear, thin voice "Good luck."

Her voice was clearer than they had heard for a long time. They both turn around and gave her a big smile.

"Today is a good day," she said firmly, with some effort.

She was in much better spirits than yesterday. The rest and warmth seemed to be helping her. Her injury was getting better. They were not sure of the specific reasons for her improvement but she was undoubtedly better.

"It is a good day," said the intuitive Jelina.

When Mondeus and Jelina looked at the landing site where they had carved the HELP sign in the sand they were quite surprised. And distressed. They had taken nearly two hours the previous day to make such a large sign. Much to their dismay, there were barely traces of it now. They had not realized that there was so much overnight wind on Riad. Their sign was almost entirely gone. Even though they sort of expected this they were surprised. And the unspoken thought came into their heads almost simultaneously. *For how many days would we have to do this?*

Mondeus was a quick thinker though. In the absence of Xander he had had become much more practical.

"Jelina, I will help you with the first two letters," he stated.

She looked at him questioningly, waiting for him to go on.

"When you are on the third letter, I'll try to find stones, pieces of wood, anything that will not blow away."

She was following.

"And mark out our sign. Even if we do one letter each day, we can have something more lasting," he explained.

It was slow tedious work. But they were motivated and continued on with purpose.

* * * * *

Balkan Villanova was silent for most of the trip to Riad. The Search and Rescue ship was quite large and equipped with all manners of gadgets and sensors, most of which he did not understand. The Deputy of Security of Aqualon, who was so quiet in the meeting on Aqualon, seemed like a different person now. Deputy Magellin was busy giving instructions and orders to the crew. Going over details of protocol and considering different possibilities. Trying to narrow the search area by pinning down the more likely landing sites, from the scant information they had gleaned.

Balkan had initially sat in with them. After a while he chose not to as there were seemingly cold discussions about what to do in the event that the young teens were seriously injured or dead. Whilst he knew this was part of the overall procedures, he could not detach himself enough to even consider those possibilities. Like any father, he remained hopeful that all was well.

They had left for Riad a couple of hours earlier. They were not expecting to get to the rocky moon until the pre-dawn hours. Their course was not exact as they were not heading for a landing port. Deputy Magellin had a fair idea of the area where the Pelican 25 had previously landed. This was obtained from the automated flight plans that were filed before the Pelican 25 had left Aqualon. The Pelican 25 database would have recorded the exact landing site. But they could not access that now. If the Pelican 25 was still on Riad, they would have been able to latch on to its locator beam and find it relatively easily. As the situation stood, they would have to comb through several hundred square miles to locate the stranded visitors. And that was if their calculations were accurate to within a ten mile radius! Deputy Magellin had no illusion that this could be a long and difficult search.

Balkan knew that they needed a bit of luck to find Jelina, Mondeus and Arielle. And even more luck to find them in a short period of time. He was hoping that they still had short range communication. This would greatly help when the Search and Rescue ship got close to Riad or when they landed. For some reason the electromagnetic field of this moon was very strong and communication was fairly difficult. It must have to do with its rocky nature and out jutting poles.

Balkan's brain refused to consider that they were not alive. What troubled him most was the fact that Xander was alone on the Pelican 25. Because of the time period involved, Xander must have been away from the rest of the group for several days now. What had caused them to be separated was the question he found most distressing. He knew that the Pelican 25 had limited passenger capability. Did the Aliens really take Xander as a hostage? And what had become of Jelina, Mondeus and Arielle? Xander had clearly stated that Jelina was still on Riad. He had made no mention of Mondeus or Arielle. Should he read between the lines? Did it imply that Mondeus and Arielle were on Riad too? Or was it just Jelina alone? Was it just the fact that Xander had limited time to pass information on to them?

His thoughts were interrupted by the announcement that Riad was now visible without the telescopic lens. Still a couple hundred thousand miles away but with the speed of these ships, they should be there in less than two hours. Magellin had one last meeting with his crew. He was outlining how they would take several aerial sweeps before landing. After landing, they would split up in three groups and proceed with small all terrain land vehicles. Balkan Villanova would stay with Magellin's party. One of the other parties was headed by one of Magellin's assistant who was at the briefing with Chief Papuan. Balkan did not know his name. They would fan out radially and be in contact at all times.

As Riad got closer, Balkan was already examining the moon's surface with the highest power telescopic lens. For anything that would give them a clue. Magellin's crew was quite understanding. But they knew that it was not possible to get that kind of details from this distance, even with their most powerful lens. Balkan's eyes ached with the effort. Yet he persisted. They were getting closer with each minute. Ironically, it got darker as they got closer. The moon was rotating away from the suns and they could not outstrip it. He finally pulled himself away from the telescopic lens.

"We will cruise and circle for about an hour before we land," Deputy Magellin informed him.

"It will be light again by then," Balkan agreed. He was an astronomer after all.

Magellin nodded.

"I have pinpointed a landing site that we will use," Magellin continued.

"I guess for now all we can do is to use the scanners and blast communication signals," Balkan said resignedly.

"We have also alerted all visitors to this moon to be on the lookout since yesterday. I will repeat that alert shortly. Got to say though, there have not been too many of them in the last couple of weeks or so," Magellin added.

"Thanks." Balkan did not know what else to say. Anything that would increase their chances was good.

The Search and Rescue ship had made at least half a dozen passes in the high probability areas with no luck. Initially it was dark but that did not affect the scanners. Blast communications on a wide range of frequencies did not pick up anything either. Balkan was noticeably anxious. This was not lost on Magellin who came over once more to inform him that they were going to land in a few minutes. Balkan already knew this but appreciated the effort.

As Magellin gave final instructions to the crew on a landing site, Balkan's eyes were still glued to the lens.

And then he saw it. Very faint at first, but rapidly taking shape as they approached the surface of the moon. Some kind of writing in the sand! He rubbed his eyes and looked again. He was sure of it now. It looked like letters.

He made out a "H" at first. And then what he thought looked like an "E". They were dancing and it was similar to reading an optician's chart.

And the lower part of a "L". There it was. Part of the word HELP!

He cried out to Magellin. One of the crew members picked it up too. It was unmistakable. And getting larger by the second. By the time Magellin came over, it was clearly visible. The Search and Rescue ship was heading directly for the letters. It was the exact location that Magellin had picked out for his ship to land.

Balkan felt a long breath escape his lungs. It had to be them. It could only be them. And they were alive, he was sure. He felt that his cheek was wet but did not know how it became so. The geography was correct. Magellin's men had been quite fastidious in their calculations. They had gone over the probabilities several times. They had concluded that this area was the likeliest location that the Pelican 25 had landed a couple of weeks earlier. The predominant question in Balkan's mind now was how long ago that sign had been written. For some reason, unsupported by real evidence, he knew it was very recent.

VI.

Chief Papuan was there early. Very early by his standards. Almost a full hour before the Pelican 25 was expected to land. He had made the short trip over from his headquarters to the spaceport still considering possibilities outside of their current plan.

There were several dozen Officers mobilized for this task. Some of them were concealed and some visible. All were surrounding the spaceport that the Pelican 25 had departed from a couple of weeks earlier. All were fully armed. Chief Papuan did not expect any trouble. The Pelican 25 was being escorted very closely all the way back. And it had not deviated at all from its projected return course to Aqualon. Yet his job was to prepare for trouble. He had several emergency teams on standby. Medical teams. Fire teams and all other supporting staff. It should be a short wait but he knew it would seem long under the circumstances.

Papuan was a man of action. He had risen though the ranks because of his excellent diplomatic skills. But his default mode was not one of inaction. In stressful situations like this one, he tended to regress to his default mode. He paced alongside the spaceport to consume the extra energy. He had his commander of the armed Officers on site and thus Papuan was not expected to direct any possible combat operations. He almost wished he was. That would have occupied him.

His main priority was the safety of Xander Villanova. He was also very much hoping that they would not have to storm the ship. That would increase the probability of injury to the hostage. He knew that that posed the greatest risk, with the possible exception of a crash landing. That would endanger all of the occupants of the Pelican 25.

Papuan also had another lingering thought at the back of his mind. He had briefly discussed this with his third in command, now that Magellin had gone to Riad. Suppose the Aliens had weapons technology superior to theirs and decided to engage in combat when they landed. They had touched on it briefly. His second Deputy thought it was unlikely. The reasons he gave were all good but Papuan was not 100 per cent convinced. The Deputy had argued that if the Aliens had such superior technology they would have mounted an offence against the Patrol ships. That did not happen. Or they would have been able to retake control of the core systems of the Pelican 25 and change its course. That also did not happen. Yet they had agreed to bring in twice the force that they would have normally for an operation of this kind.

The thought did cross Papuan's mind as to whether they were they being extra cautious or fearful. He was honest enough to admit that a bit of fear had crept into their minds. Fear was not a logical thing. Papuan knew that. And fear of the unknown was even less understood. Papuan understood the reasons for his, yet he could do very little about it. An involuntary smile crossed his lips. Ten to twenty years ago, fear would have never entered his mind. He would have looked at this as a great opportunity. To prove his skills and to enhance his career. Yes, the power of youth and exuberance, he reflected. Or was that the ignorance of youth? He decided to settle on the caution of experience.

The Officers knew Papuan was nervous. Those close to him had seen this pacing before. He flashed an occasional smile but his eyes remained steely. He had a personal stake in this too. If he botched this, he was almost certain that the Head of the Ixodia system would replace him. In the last 24-48 hours, this story had gotten into the media and everyone was following it as it unfolded. In fact, he had had to cordon off this entire area from civilians earlier in the day.

Chief Papuan mentally reviewed their situation one more time. They knew that the Pelican 25 was not carrying more than ten men at the absolute maximum. It was not built for this. Perhaps they could fit in a dozen for low speed travel. For distant travel, it just did not have the capacity. If the Aliens were reasoning people and wanted to survive, they would surrender without a battle. But he also knew that desperate people often lose their ability to reason.

Papuan felt a light tap on his shoulder. One of his Officers whispered to him. The Pelican 25 was in range. "In range" in this case meant that it could fire a weapon into Aqualon. It would only be a few more minutes before they could see it based on its speed. Some of the members on his force were tracking it on radar. Papuan refused to stare into a screen all the time. He would wait. He trusted his instincts. All his men were in position. Waiting. Tense. Heads looking up and arms extended with fully loaded weapons. For the umpteenth time, Papuan hoped that this would be non violent.

And then he saw it too. First a tiny speck in the sky. Then three more specks. Rapidly getting larger. Heading directly for them. The Patrol Ships had now moved to the rear of the Pelican 25. A murmur from his Officers. Then everyone felt silent. All in their predetermined position.

Papuan let out his first deep breath in more than half an hour. He saw the Pelican 25 starting to decelerate. The ships in the sky were not getting larger at a constant rate anymore. The increase in size had slowed relative to time. The first hurdle seemed to have been scaled. The Pelican 25 was still functioning well. And it now appeared that it would not crash land. He was sure that his well trained force had picked that up too. Even before radar confirmation. Maybe the emergency support teams would have an easy day after all. As the fire and medical teams eased back into the perimeters of the spaceport, more of the combat teams moved forward.

VII.

The hospital had given them a special suite. They were technically visitors to Aqualon and now that all of Aqualon and most of Ixodia had heard about them on the news, every courtesy was being extended. The hospital administrator himself had ensured that they got everything they needed. There was a very large sitting room at the end of the patient room. Adjacent to the main waiting room were sleeping quarters that were no less luxurious than any top-class hotel room. All of this was located in the penthouse level of Aqualon's largest hospital, less than a half hour travel from where the Pelican 25 first landed.

Erik and Nandie Carmical sat on either side of the bed. Their patient had undergone surgery earlier in the day and had been sleeping for the last few hours. Arielle Carmical opened her eyes slowly. She rubbed them as one who still could not separate out her long series of dreams on Riad and her current reality. Perhaps some of the side effects of anesthesia. Or remnants of the sedative she had on the trip back from Riad, which were not helping her cause either.

Her parents holding both of her hands was no illusion though.

"How are you feeling dear?" Nandie Carmical asked.

"Sleepy," she smiled thinly.

"Your doctor said you will be sleepy for a few hours after the surgery," Erik Carmical added.

"Can we get you anything?" Nandie asked.

"I am starving," Arielle said.

Nandie and Erik looked at each other delighted and then at their watches. It was almost three hours since her surgery. Her doctor did say she could eat three to four hours after.

"I'll call it in," Erik said. He pressed a button on the panel at the bedside for food services.

Hearing the conversation, Xander moved across the room from the sitting area. Mondeus and Jelina pulled their chairs over too. And soon they were followed by Balkan Villanova. One by one they gave Arielle a tight hug. No words, just a hug. It had been a long couple of weeks. So much had happened in just the last thirty six hours alone. And Arielle did not even know all the details.

Xander was ready to fill Arielle in when she was ready. Mondeus could not wait. He had asked Xander a thousand questions since they were reunited. Jelina was thankful they were all together and well again. Just feeling the happy emotions were enough for her at this time. The atmosphere satiated her needs. Details could come later.

As the attendant brought in a packed tray of food, Balkan Villanova was having a quiet conversation with Erik Carmical. The Carmicals had gotten in via commercial travel early this morning. They got to Aqualon just prior to Arielle's surgery. They were able to be with her for a short time before the surgery. Their comfort and reassurance was invaluable. The surgery had taken less than two hours, Erik was saying. The doctors had to fuse a bone in Arielle's ankle to stabilize her foot. First, they had had to shave off part of the bone as it had been seeded by bacteria and was probably infected. The doctors explained to the Carmicals after the surgery, that the broken bones had already begun to heal on their own. But they were mal-aligned which meant that Arielle would walk with a limp if they did not intervene. At the surgery they separated the bones, debrided them and fused them together with the addition of a special bone cement.

"How much longer would she need to stay in hospital?" Balkan asked.

"I can answer that," a booming voice came from the open doorway of the Suite. Arielle's chief orthopedic surgeon made his way over to the bedside to check on his most recent patient.

"Ready to run a marathon?" he asked Arielle in that over the top positive attitude of his.

"Next week," Arielle smiled.

"I would wait until next year," he continued cheerfully.

Turning to the Carmicals and sounding just a bit more serious he continued,

"She will need ultrasonic treatment daily for the next three to five days. This will accelerate healing. She will also get daily antimicrobials."

"When can we travel doctor?" Nandie Carmical was as polite ever.

"Anytime, after that, I suppose."

Nandie was every bit as intuitive as Jelina. She sense some reluctance in the "I suppose."

"What is your preference doctor?" she asked courteously.

Arielle's doctor flashed a broad smile. He knew that the Carmicals wanted to get back to The System as soon as possible, so Arielle would miss very little school. He was being given an easy way out to express his honest recommendations.

"I would prefer her to wait for a week before long range travel," he said.

"A week it will be, doctor," Erik Carmical assured him with finality in his voice.

"Great. I will see you first thing tomorrow. Surgeons do start early in the morning," he added as he squeezed Arielle's shoulder gently.

"Thank you doctor," Arielle said softly.

* * * * *

Mondeus was already asking Xander more questions before the doctor was scarcely out of the room. Arielle took a few ravenous bites. Nonchalantly, Mondeus plucked a bit of food from Arielle's tray and put it into his mouth without even asking. Jelina and Mrs. Carmical both smiled. Things were returning to normal quickly.

"And what happened after the Pelican 25 touched down?" Mondeus persisted.

Xander had already given him a synopsis of the events but Mondeus wanted more details. This time Arielle wanted to hear it too. She was aware that Xander had been taken hostage. She was also told that he was expected back on Aqualon before long. This was just after they departed from Riad. And just before they gave her a sedative on the trip back.

Soon after Dr. Villanova, Deputy Magellin and his team had landed on Riad, the medics from the Search and Rescue squad took over. Magellin and crew had confirmation just before their ship landed. Mondeus and Tytum had picked up a communication. And had responded. As Jelina and Mondeus were running outside, the ship had landed. The team did not even have to look for them. They landed in the same clearing of the original landing site of the Pelican 25. Just next to the letters that Mondeus and Jelina had tediously carved out in the sand. Arms waving, Mondeus and Jelina greeted them. They were hugely surprised to see Balkan Villanova. Jelina just jumped into her father's arms as he hugged her tightly. Tears of joy and relief flowed freely from both of them. Balkan also reached out an arm for Mondeus.

The medical team quickly brought a real stretcher for Arielle. And deftly carried her to the ship. Once aboard, they had given her intravenous fluids and antibiotics. And a sedative for her to get some rest. The ship was well equipped to deal with medical situations.

Deputy Magellin had relayed the news to Aqualon. Chief Papuan had taken the opportunity to inform Dr. Villanova that Xander's landing was imminent. They were in constant communication with Aqualon. Balkan was comforted to have his daughter and Mondeus with him. But he remained anxious for Xander's well being. As were Jelina and Mondeus.

After that, Arielle remembered seeing Xander briefly before her surgery. She thought she had also seen him the evening before but her memory was fuzzy because of the sedation. She was sure, however, that he was there along with her parents and Mondeus and Jelina prior to her undergoing anesthesia. And what a surprise that had been. To wake up very early that morning and see her parents on Aqualon. She squeezed their hands tightly again. She was more alert now. She felt stronger now that she had eaten. And more energized than she had been for a long time.

"I want to know too," Arielle said as she looked at Xander.

"Well," Xander said.

He was just so glad to be speaking to her again. He could not deny her the request. So much had happened since he left her injured and went looking for help. Many times he had thought he would never get a chance to relate this experience to her. And a few of those times were before he was captured.

"Well, in many ways, landing again on Aqualon was more uneventful than most of the trip. Of course, I was scared. I didn't know what Bodak and his crew would do. Just before we landed, they had a group discussion. It seemed as if the crew convinced Bodak and Mordak to surrender. When we landed, they were all silent and resigned for a while. We could see clearly from inside the Pelican 25 that we were completely surrounded by security forces. To resist at that stage did not make sense. Even to Bodak."

"But it was you who told them to put their hands in the air and leave the spaceship?" Mondeus prompted somewhat gleefully. He seemed to enjoy that part a lot.

"Technically, I was relaying a message from Chief Papuan," Xander continued. Balkan Villanova looked at Mondeus and smiled understandingly. He was still a youngster. Jelina just rubbed the back of Mondeus's neck playfully. They had been through a lot. And she knew for a lifetime to come that Mondeus could be serious if the situation dictated it. Arielle just gazed at Xander wide eyed.

"Go on," Arielle urged.

"After we landed, Bodak opened the communication channels. Chief Papuan was saying that no one would be hurt if the Gadorans would put their hands in the air and exited the ship in a single file. They could not understand. So I used the translator to relay the message," Xander explained.

"And they followed your instructions," Mondeus beamed. He just could not get enough of this.

"Chief Papuan said they were worried about you for a short while. Why did you come out last?" Jelina asked her brother.

"I guess as the hostage they expected me to be first," Xander said referring to Papuan. "I waited because Hadik's brother was still aboard. He needed help."

Balkan Villanova knew he had raised a good son. Even in his time of highest stress, he showed compassion for others. Balkan was very proud of him.

There was a light knock at the door and large figure loomed in the doorway.

"Can I come in folks?" Chief Papuan asked.

"Sure Chief," Balkan Villanova answered.

"You can do anything on this moon," Balkan added coyly.

"Just checking. This is civilian territory."

Papuan was back to his diplomatic best. Balkan had developed a deep respect for Papuan after being with him for the last few days. His judgment was excellent and he was as sharp as a tack.

"Just wanted to drop by briefly and say hi," Papuan said as he shook hands with the Carmicals.

"We are very thankful for the job you have done here Chief," Balkan volunteered in a more sober tone.

"My duty," he nodded.

"Please extend our thanks to Deputy Magellin and his team as well."

"I will." Balkan knew that the Chief's type did not do too well with compliments. They became uncomfortable, so he did not persist.

"When are you returning to the system?" Papuan asked.

"As soon as the Pelican 25 is ready," Balkan said.

"The Carmicals will be here for another week whilst Arielle recuperates," Balkan added looking in their direction as they nodded in agreement.

"Well I have good news. The Pelican 25 would be ready by tomorrow."

"Great."

"It checked out fairly well. Our engineering team found no major core damage. They are working on refitting it with some of its original technology that the Gadorans had modified. They will take it for a test ride before returning it to you."

"Then we can leave the day after tomorrow?" Balkan looked at Xander and Mondeus for approval. They nodded reluctantly. They had to return to school next week. But it was good to have Dr Villanova with them on their return trip to The System.

"I will personally see you off," Papuan said.

"No need to Chief," Balkan protested weakly as Papuan turned to leave.

"It will be my pleasure," the Chief boomed in a voice that few people objected to.

* * * * *

It must have been the day for visitors. A few minutes after Chief Papuan left there was another knock on the door. This time it was two men. A uniformed Officer and another shorter man.

"Come in," the Carmicals said, even though they did not recognize them.

"Hadik!" Xander exclaimed joyfully.

"Xander!" Hadik said happily as they shook hands.

Introductions were made. Only Balkan seemed fully at ease with Hadik. The others were not sure how to interact with him. Xander had spent several hours the night before describing in detail his experience as a captive on the Pelican 25 to his father. Jelina also heard most of it. Jelina also went into the details of their experiences on Riad over the last couple of weeks. Mondeus was present but was so exhausted that he missed some pieces of it, as his body forced him to sleep. Xander had delineated to his father how considerate Hadik was to him.

The Officer with Hadik was more of a guide than for security reasons. He left after informing Hadik that he would be back in an hour. Because there was no translator, there was a silence after the initial "How do you do?"

Balkan Villanova saw that Xander was taller than Hadik. He also noted the features of Hadik and was reminded of a field internship he did many many years ago, during his University years. A group of them were posted on a remote planet outpost for a few months. The local people had features with some resemblance to the Gadorans. After a few months he learnt quite a bit of the local language. On a hunch, he spoke to Hadik in that language.

To their amazement, Hadik broke into a big grin and responded joyfully. Hadik spoke several languages. Even though it was not one of his native languages, he was skillful in this one. It was common in a System that the Gadoran people were familiar with.

"When do you go back to your System?" Dr. Villanova asked.

"Gadin and the others leave next week. As you know it is a very long way away. They have to travel to two intermediary relay stations to get there. And there is travel only about once every two weeks from here," Hadik explained.

"And you?" Dr. Villanova asked, after he informed the rest of the group of what Hadik was saying

"I will stay here with my brother for the next fours weeks or so. Until he is well enough to travel. The doctors say he is already making rapid progress with your medicines."

Xander felt warmth in his chest as his father relayed the message.

Chief Papuan had spoken to Balkan Villanova the night before. Balkan already knew the plight of some of the Gadorans. There was a hearing the same day that they were taken prisoners. The Judicial Council, after a couple of hours of deliberation, went fairly light on them. Extenuating circumstances were the reason. They had decided that Hadik and his brother could stay as long as necessary for his brother to recover. Gadin and the rest of the Gadorans were free to leave when transport was available. There would be a formal reprimand and documentation of this event would be tagged to their identity. Bodak and Mordak would be detained on Aqualon for a period of three to six months until discussions were had with the Gadoran people. The Gadoran system would decide their final fate in keeping with their culture and laws.

"I will like to thank you for the compassion that you showed my son on that very difficult trip," Balkan said.

"You are welcome. Your people and people here on Aqualon have been most gracious and forgiving to us. If in some way, we had been able to communicate with them before, all of this would have never occurred," Hadik said, bowing his head slightly.

Balkan knew that Hadik was again apologizing for the recent events. The Gadorans had lived through many years of futility. No need for him or anyone to be too harsh on them now. They had already paid their dues.

As Balkan was conversing, he had a strange flashback. He thought of his missing wife. As they were trying to figure out the relay stations last night for the Gadoran's return trip, the second stopover seemed vaguely familiar. A sudden insight made him realized the reason. It was in that general area, that his wife's ship was last calculated to have been. They had completed their mission and after leaving the distant planet, had never turned up at the next transit station. Models of speed and communication timelines had worked out that they were last in that general area. Of course, that general area spanned several million miles. With nothing else to go on and given the remoteness of that area of the galaxy not much could be done. They were never heard from again and were presumed to have had a fatal malfunction or accident.

"Why didn't you help Xander escape?" The question came from Mondeus and was as direct as ever. Balkan thought it was somewhat rude but he reworded it politely and translated it.

Hadik did not seem to mind and was very forthcoming with an answer.

"According to our laws, disobeying the orders of a commanding Officer of a ship a very serious crimes and carries a severe punishment," Hadik explained.

"I wanted to help Xander as much as possible, but there was only so much I could do."

Xander nodded. He had witnessed the authority of Bodak first hand.

"I do have something to ask you Hadik," he started haltingly, with his father translating.

"Go on," Hadik urged.

"Were you aware that I reset the ship's course from the secondary terminals upstairs?"

Hadik first looked at the floor and then looked directly at Xander. Everyone in the room was looking at him.

"Yes," he said quietly.

"Why didn't you tell the others?"

"I knew my brother could not survive the long trip. It was the only hope for him to live," Hadik explained.

"I was hoping that you would do something. That is why I left you without the handcuffs."

"I understand now." The words came from the lips of both Xander and Balkan Villanova slowly.

They exchanged looks. In many ways the Gadorans were more similar to them than different. They all realized now that they owed their survival to Hadik as much as anyone else. Even Mondeus understood the gravity of what was just said.

Arielle finally broke the silence.

"Perhaps we could visit your System one day," she offered.

"Great idea," Mondeus agreed.

"It would be my privilege and honor to host all of you," Hadik said.

"It would be a pleasure," Xander replied.

"We would love to see your world and culture," Jelina added.

Xander and Jelina sitting on either side of their father with Mondeus and the Carmicals on either side of Arielle made a pretty picture. Balkan was not yet ready to think about another long trip much less discuss it. Jelina sensed this and squeezed her father's hand tightly. Arielle and Mondeus exchanged a similar reaction with her parents. Xander smiled understandingly, knowing such a trip would be a long way in the future.